The Glory to Come:
Revelation
and the
Triumph of Christ

By

DENNIS RICHARD MAHONEY, Ph.D. M.A, MBA

Table of Contents

Preface

Have you ever thought you have little to offer to and little to say to the Lord God of us all? You would be wrong to think this. You have what God desires most: your prayers of gratitude and praise, and your fidelity. *The Revelation to John* teaches us how to pray.

When you sing praise to the boundless glory, endless power, and unlimited goodness of God; when you reflect on the magnificence of God's creation; and when you sit in silence, you are in His presence. The offering you make to God in those moments is what He seeks from you. He seeks your worship. Worship is what you will be doing endlessly in heaven. To master prayer, focus on what God wants. We are told throughout Scripture what He wants, and it is clear and easy to offer: forever sing praise to the Lord your God. Do not focus on what you want, focus on the majesty of God. Do this, and you will be raised up to our loving God.   He will give you what you need.   We are taught this truth throughout the Bible. Prayer is what God wants most from us. Pray by praising Him for His greatness, goodness, and mercy. This is how every Christian should pray—pleasing Him, just as He asks. You will read in *Revelation* how the saints and the angels pray in heaven. For inspiration and guidance, look to the example of the saved Christians praying night and day in heaven, praising God for His glory and greatness.

Are you just starting? Do you marvel and feel a sense of wonder when you gaze upon the oceans, mountains, and forests? Do the living creatures of the earth seem majestic to you? Perhaps wild horses, or whales, or hummingbirds give you a sense of awe. God created them all.

We need not, and should not, pray for fulfillment of our needs from God. He knows what we truly need before we ask. We only need to thank God for His mercy and praise Him for His endless goodness and greatness. God knows, and He cares.

Our calling is to be with God—starting in silence if we must—and to respond when our hearts guide us to sing endless praises of His glory. In the Bible's final Word, the beautiful book The Revelation to John, we are shown in detail what heaven will be like. It will be an indescribably joyous eternity with God.

Sadly, many preachers and pastors do not preach Revelation or present it to their congregations with fidelity to how it is written. There is nothing unclear and nothing frightening in this final book from God. It is a glorious final message that exudes hope and love.

Our task is to read and believe. We know that Christ will return to earth, and that He is coming soon. He tells us this over and over again. We know that Christ will come to defeat Satan, his agents, and all unrepentant sinners – and their defeat will be complete, inescapable. We know that we are all sinners and that Christ has died for our sins. Until we receive our perfected bodies and are carried up to heaven, we will know suffering. Countless martyrs have died for their faith. Christians often know pain and suffering—so did Jesus the Christ. The faithful who endure to the end will be rewarded with eternal life. Believers will no longer know pain when we are resurrected.

The final days will be primarily for Jesus, our Lord and our God, to punish the wicked and to perfect the Jews, who are God's people. Unrepentant sinners will have it very hard. God's justice will come swiftly. Our salvation will also be swift.

In His mercy, Jesus will "rescue" believers by rapturing His church of believers up to the clouds of heaven before God's justice is poured out on sinners. *The Gift of Salvation: Will You Be Raised Up to the Clouds of Heaven?*, my first book, traces God's Word from Genesis through the creation of the new heaven and the new earth. Believers will be spared from the days of suffering. God's justice will be delivered quickly. In but one hour, Christ will forever defeat Satan and triumph with His angels in the battle of Armageddon.

Does this sound fantastic? It is. What is truly fantastic is that this will happen. It is exactly what the Bible says. The Bible is God's sacred Word and His indescribable gift of love. Join me, please, in a walk through the climactic last book of the Bible: The Revelation to John.

Chapter 1

The Culmination of the Bible

The Revelation to John is the culmination of the Bible. It is the last chapter and the last recorded Words of God in sacred Scripture. This revelation of the triumphant second coming of Jesus Christ, our Lord and Savior, was given to the Son by God the Father and delivered to the apostle John by God's angel. Revelation begins: "The revelation of Jesus Christ, which God gave him to show to his servants the things that must soon take place. He made it known by sending his angel to his servant John." (Revelation 1:1).

In the original Greek text, the word for "Revelation" is apokalupsis, translated as an "uncovering," "disclosure," or "unveiling." It refers to the unveiling of spiritual truth or events, such as the incarnation of Christ (Romans 8:19; 16:25; Galatians 1:12; Ephesians 1:17; 3:3; Luke 2:32). The Revelation to John reveals the End of Times—the second coming of Jesus to judge sinners, and the promise of the new heaven and new earth.

These final Words from God were given to John, the disciple whom Jesus loved, during his exile on Patmos, a desolate volcanic island in the Aegean Sea off the coast of modern Turkey. Patmos, forty miles offshore, was a Roman penal colony where prisoners labored in mines.

John was in his late eighties at the time. The emperor Titus Flavius Domitian banished him for refusing to worship Domitian, as all subjects were required to do. Domitian intended to silence John, but God had other plans. In exile, John received and recorded God's Revelation, transforming

Domitian's attempt at suppression into God's channel for the church's encouragement. The message of Revelation is simple and enduring: remain faithful to the end. While Rome fell, the church endured and grew.

Under Roman guard, John was poorly fed, ill-clothed, and forced to sleep on the bare ground. During his confinement, Domitian persecuted Christians throughout Asia. After Domitian's Death, John was released and returned to Ephesus.

In the years after the Crucifixion, Rome regarded Christians as a branch of Judaism, not a separate religion. This is clear in the rulings of Gallio, chief judicial officer in A.D. 51–52 (Acts 18:12–16). Later, when Rome declared Christianity distinct from Judaism, it was ruled illegal. Persecution did not begin immediately, but in A.D. 64, Emperor Nero, seeking a scapegoat for the great fire he caused, blamed Christians. From that moment, persecution spread throughout the empire. Many innocent believers were executed, and John, along with others, suffered.

Some thirty years later, Domitian ordered the persecution of Christians across the empire, including Asia. By then, John was the only living apostle, and he was exiled. The church, facing hardship and uncertainty, needed guidance and strength. It was in this setting that John received the vision and recorded it in Revelation.

The early church thought Jesus would soon return. The Revelation to John begins by telling the church that "the time is near." This last book of the Bible is prophetic: it tells us about the coming return of Jesus Christ, the Lord of lords and the King of kings. Some readers find prophetic books daunting, complex, and confusing. The key to understanding is to simply read and reflect on the sacred text.

A prophecy is a vision or a message from God to the prophet of something that will happen in the future. These divinely inspired messages tell us of what is to come or declare God's will. Prophecy informs spiritual understanding and righteousness. John recorded "all that he saw" (Revelation 1:2), which included a trip to heaven and messages delivered through an angel.

God informs us of what we need to know. The Lord wants us to understand and obey His Word. The angel sent by God (Revelation 1:1) spoke clearly and vividly to John of what is to come at the end of times. Believers are called to accept God's Word, and His Word is always clear. Why would the Lord want His people to be confused?

The Words of God's angel and John's vision of heaven were spiritually rich and glorious. Revelation reveals God our Father in all His glory, majesty, power, and faithfulness. It is humbling that He who is all-powerful is completely faithful to His creation. Within Revelation, we see both the depths of human depravity and the promises of redemption and salvation. The Prologue declares: "Blessed is the one who reads aloud the words of this prophecy, and blessed are those who hear, and who keep what is written in it, for the time is near" (Revelation 1:3). In verse 1:5 we are given the great promise of the Almighty Lord Jesus the Christ, the "ruler of kings on earth…who loves us and has freed us from our sins by His Blood." Jesus the Christ will save His church, and believers will be spared the punishing judgments of the Lord our God.

Revelation is the powerful and inspirational culmination of God's written Word. The great revealing begins in chapters 4–5, where John records his extraordinary vision of heaven. Scripture contains just two accounts of believers permitted to see heaven in visions. The first is Paul's account in 2 Corinthians 12 of being transported to the "third heaven," the innermost sanctuary of God. Paul was forbidden to report what he saw. John, however, was commanded to provide a detailed account of his vision, including his actual trip to heaven when he was commanded "come up here" (Revelation 4:1). Chapter 4 begins the unfolding of John's vivid description of the gates of heaven opened before him.

When symbolism is used in the text, it is explained in the text. For example, the seven lampstands in Revelation 1:12 are said to represent the seven churches to whom John was writing. Symbolism can also be clarified by Old Testament writings. John saw things he had never encountered before and had to describe in words what the angel showed him. To guide us, Jesus presented the revelations to John in three ways: as things seen in the past, existing in the present, and to take place in the future. The Lord always helps His people to understand His Word.

The main message of this book is that believers are to remain faithful to Jesus despite persecution, for Christ is coming again soon to bring salvation to the righteous and eternal punishment to the wicked.

I have never suffered persecution for my faith. Yet around the world today, many Christians are jailed, beaten, tortured, and killed. Sin prevails, and Satan can seem indefatigable and unconquerable. Believers must guard against being misled or distracted by evil or spiritual trials. The Revelation to John calls us to be ready, because Jesus is coming again soon.

And what will become of believers? We are told exactly in The Revelation to John: we will be so blessed.

> "Many Christians have been taught that we will spend eternity floating around someplace. But the Bible teaches that our primary residence for eternity will be the earth, which will be restored and recreated to the state God originally intended. In the new heaven and new earth, God will "wipe away every tear from (our) eyes; and there will no longer be any Death. There will be no longer any mourning, or crying, or pain; the first things have passed away" (Bible Prophecy Made Simple, Dr. Robert Jeffress, Pathway to Victory, 2020, p. 24.).

Revelation begins by telling us that it is the "revelation of Jesus Christ which God gave Him to show to his servants the things that soon must take place. He made it known by sending his angel to his servant John, who bore witness to the Word of God and to the testimony of Jesus Christ, even to all that he saw. Blessed is the one who reads aloud the words of this prophecy, and blessed are those who hear, and who keep what is written in it, for the time is near." (Revelation 1:1-3).

This book lifts the veil on God's unseen interventions, forces, and angels that have been operating from the beginning of time, and tells of the events and outcomes that await us. Revelation ties together all that the Lord has revealed to His creation. Over fifty percent of its verses refer to the Old Testament, including Exodus, Psalms, Isaiah, Jeremiah, Ezekiel, Daniel, and Zechariah. Revelation is the ultimate book in Scripture and the fulfilment of the Old Testament prophecies regarding Jesus. The Old Testament makes 1,800 references to the triumphant second coming of Jesus. Revelation is His last Word prior to His return. Although the exact date of its writing is unknown, most Biblical scholars circle around A.D. 95–96.

Beginning in Chapter 2, John writes to the seven churches of Asia: Ephesus, Smyrna, Pergamum, Thyatira, Sardis, Philadelphia, and Laodicea, churches that John knew well. He had spent time with them teaching the Word. Some were struggling with sin and false teachings while others were growing in discipleship.

Revelation was also written as a blessing for those who read it. God ends the Bible, His book, with a blessing to those who read it. The text is presented in full for your ease, quoting the English Standard Version, 2008 edition, a widely accepted version and more "readable" than the King James.

Still to this day, we will be blessed by God if we read His Words in Revelation. By reading the Biblical text within, God promises His blessing. God states His promise to us in the text itself.

The second coming of Christ will be the time of final judgment. Sinners will be cast into the Lake of Fire, which is hell. Preachers and people do not like to speak of hell these days. Hell is real. But it is not there for you. If you are reading this book, you are a believer. Believers and those who come to Christ during the Great Tribulation will be "saved up" to a joyous heaven for eternity. The reality of the Second Coming and final judgment can be difficult for some to believe, but it is God's sacred Word. Because of this, some readers struggle, some are fearful, some do not heed the Word, and some redefine it to suit their desired outcomes. Such are dangerous responses. All we need to do is accept God's Word as given to us. We can rejoice that because we are believers, we will be saved.

If you are uncertain or struggling, simply do this: read, accept what you read, and ask God to help you in your acceptance and understanding of that which is true. Sometimes we need to rely on faith and trust, which is actually the best thing we can do. When we respond this way, struggle evaporates and peace is ours. It helps to take time to reflect on the miracles that have occurred in our lives. Things have happened to all of us that cannot be explained by human understanding.

While the time of the return of Jesus Christ is imminent, it is imminent in God's time. The Almighty's time is unknown to man, and even unknown to His Son. Jesus told his disciples: "But concerning that day and hour, no one knows, not even the angels of heaven, nor the Son, but the Father only" (Matt. 24:36). In Greek, the words for "taking place soon" are en tachei, which suggests that when the events of Revelation do begin, they will happen quickly. Jesus repeatedly told His disciples to always be watchful and ready. Once the End of Times begins, the prophecy will unfold over seven years.

Once again, while some struggle with the book of Revelation, as with all Scripture, the reader only needs to accept what is written as it is written. John MacArthur wrote, "The late British Prime Minister Winston Churchill once described the former Soviet Union as 'a riddle wrapped in a mystery inside an enigma.'" (Because the Time is Near,

Moody Publishers, 2007, p.7). Some Christians view the book of Revelation in much the same way. Bewildered by its mystical symbolism and striking imagery, many believers and church leaders avoid serious study of this book. Furthermore, some readers are frightened by the Lord's punishment of sin and the defeat of Satan. Such short-sightedness deprives believers of the blessings God promises to those who diligently read this last book of Scripture.

The complete book is reprinted within this text for your easy reference. As you read Revelation, be assured that it is God's inspired Word expressed in powerful and dramatic imagery. The end-times events—the rapture, the Great Tribulation, the battle of Armageddon, and the millennium—are dramatic and powerful events that will happen. God said as much in His opening to Revelation: "Blessed is the one who reads aloud the words of this prophecy, and blessed are those who hear, and who keep what is written in it." (Revelation 1:3). I encourage you to read the passages of Revelation aloud, which was the practice of Christians in the early church. May you find this technique helpful.

As we advance through Revelation, we will see the depravity of man in vivid technicolor. During the seven-year Great Tribulation, we will see humankind with hardened hearts who refuse to repent. Even as God pours out His crushing judgment, sinners will rage in anger, but will not repent of their sin.

Chapter 2

Let's Start

Be ready. The time is near.

As you read, this terminology guide might help you. Jesus is named in many ways throughout Revelation:

◊   The faithful witness (1:5)
◊   The firstborn of the dead (1:5)
◊   The ruler of the kings of the earth (1:5)
◊   The Alpha and the Omega (1:8; 21:6)
◊   The first and the last (1:17)
◊   The living One (1:17)
◊   The one who holds the seven stars in His right hand, the One who walks among the seven golden lampstands (2:1)
◊   The One who has the sharp two-edged sword (2:12)
◊   The Son of God (2:18)
◊   The One "who has eyes like a flame of fire, and …feet…like burnished bronze" (2:18)
◊   The One "who has the seven Spirits of God and the seven stars" (3:1)
◊   The One who is holy, who is true" (3:7)
◊   The holder of the "key of David, who opens and no one will shut, and who shuts and no one opens" (3:7)
◊   The Amen, the faithful and true Witness (3:14)
◊   The Beginning of the creation of God (3:14)
◊   The Lion that is from the tribe of Judah (5:5)
◊   The Root of David (5:5)
◊   The Lamb of God (5:6; 6:1, 7:9-101; 8:1)
◊   The Lord, holy and true" (6:10)

◊ The One who is called Faithful and True" (19:11)
◊ The Word of God (19:16)
◊ King of kings, and Lord of lords (19:16)
◊ Christ (Messiah), ruling on earth with his glorified saints (20:6)
◊ The root and the descendant of David, and the bright morning star (22:16)

Perhaps a reason why Jesus is named in Revelation by so many names is to convey to us the majesty and depth of His glorious being and His dominion.

The purpose of revelation is to reveal God's truth. It tells us what our future will be as members of God's church. The same term is used in Romans 8:19, telling of the glory of the coming "revealing of the sons of God," or believers in Christ, who will have inheritance. In Romans 16:25 we read of the mystery of the revelation of spiritual truths kept secret for ages. We also read of the revelation of Christ the Son's second coming in Luke 2:32, 2 Thessalonians 1:7, and 1 Peter 1:7. Here in the Book of Revelation, we are given the final revelations—those of the full and final chapters on eternal salvation and eternal damnation.

There are different views on the Book of Revelation, held by various schools of theological thought. This author believes there is one correct view.

> "The Preterist school believes that the events of Revelation were fulfilled beginning in A.D. 70 with the Destruction of Jerusalem by the Romans. The Historicist school believes that the Book of Revelation is an overview of church history, describing various times of persecution and tribulation. The Idealist

view is that Revelation should be interpreted symbolically, as a nonliteral depiction of the battle between God and the satanic forces of evil. The Futurist understanding of Revelation is it is a prophetic account of actual future events, specifically focused on the end of this age. This view is the natural result of a straightforward reading of the book." (MacArthur, p.37).

The futurist reading is the only one consistent with a literal interpretation of Scripture. It aligns with prophecy as the descriptor of Revelation. It is not based on human opinion or interpretation, but solely on the Word of God as given to us in this sacred book.

Sometimes it is easy to be overwhelmed by the ugliness and tragedy we see daily. Scripture tells us that things will only get worse until Christ returns to crush the serpent. The Book of Revelation gives us comfort. It tells us what to expect. It gives us faith and strength in the promise of God and the ultimate triumph of our Lord Jesus Christ. May He come to us again soon.

Several key themes stand out in Revelation. The first is that Jesus the Christ conquered Satan by His sacrificial Death on the Cross, paying the ransom for all sinners. Jesus remains present among His believers and in His church through the Holy Spirit. Christ is the Lamb, the Lamb of victory. He is in control. God our Father restrains His wrath against the evil who attack His church. Although limited for now by God, wars, famine, drought, disease, and sin persist. Believers who remain faithful will conquer evil and be rewarded when Christ returns. Satan will continue his attacks and persecution of believers until the End of Times, when Christ will destroy all the enemies of earth and heaven. Then a new earth and a new heaven will replace what is destroyed and cleansed by the Lord Jesus Christ.

The Revelation begins with letters to seven churches of Asia, all well known to, and likely founded by, John. John had been with these churches, expanding and preaching to them prior to his exile on Patmos. The letters, dictated by God, are personal and specific to each church. Some churches receive great praise, others rebuke, but all receive encouragement to continue in faith and evangelization.

John writes to the seven churches to guide, praise, encourage, and in some cases, correct and admonish them. God's churches faced great persecution and challenge. God the Father and God the Son were warring with Satan and his army of demons. Jesus the Lamb defeated sin and Death on the Cross, but evil was not yet vanquished. Evil attacked the early churches, just as it does today.

Symbolism is used in Revelation. Jesus is presented as the Lamb. Churches are represented by lamps and lampstands. Satan is portrayed as a dragon with seven heads and ten horns. Symbolism is used widely throughout Scripture. Jesus used symbolism in His Olivet Discourse. The New Testament employs images and symbolism to portray moral decline, cataclysms, disasters, the tribulation, the Parousia (the second coming of Christ), the day of final judgment, and the dissolution of the earth to be replaced by the new earth. When you read the text of Revelation below, with its extraordinarily powerful and descriptive language, you will find it as vivid as if you were present with John on Patmos. Symbolism and vivid imagery convey the divine nature of Revelation and its full power—in technicolor.

The Revelation begins with what was at the time: the churches of the first century and their struggles and successes. It then moves to the things that will soon take place. Revelation builds to a great crescendo. The divine number seven repeats from the seven churches to four series of seven visions and messages: the seven seals on the scroll, the trumpets, and the seven bowls of God's wrath. God's wrath will be poured out on His enemies, who will be crushed in one hour. The church will stand forward as the bride of the Lamb in a new heaven and a new earth. Satan will be defeated in battle with Christ. In verses 12:1–6, we learn of the defeat of the dragon, which is Satan, when it sought to destroy the child of the heavenly woman, who found safety in the wilderness. The dragon is thwarted in its attacks on believers.

As you read through Revelation, you progress from what was at the time (the seven churches) to the things that will take place as Christ defends His church and defeats His enemies. Heaven will open. Christ the Lamb will receive the sacred scroll and open the seven seals. Angels will sound trumpets. The wrath of God will pour out on evil. It will be a cosmic battle between Christ and Satan. The Archangel Michael will come with the armies of heaven, and the dragon will be quickly defeated. The wrath of God will be prominently displayed. The triumph of God over evil will be complete victory.

God's wrath is real. It is fierce and terrifying, but poured out only on as the evil. Yet it is ignored by many churches today. When it is preached, many churchgoers want to deny or dismiss God's wrath. In Revelation, His wrath is reserved for Satan and the dragon. Satan was cast out of heaven long ago. Original sin in the garden of Eden brought evil into creation, and sin has been with us ever since. But God's violent wrath will not fall on believers. The church, which includes all believers living and dead, will be in heaven before the tribulation begins. They will have been raptured to heaven (please see The Gift of Salvation by Dennis Richard Mahoney). What comes after the defeat of evil by Jesus Christ and His armies is unimaginable and eternal bliss.

Following the end times will be one thousand years of peace on earth, then Christ's eternal rule and freedom from all sin and sorrow. The saved in Christ have nothing to fear and everything to look forward to. The Bible unfolds what is to come. For Satan, his demonic forces, and the wicked, what will come will be crushing defeat and eternal punishment. For Christians, there will be life in eternal bliss.

Let us begin with God's last Words to us in The Revelation to John.

Chapter 3

Prologue

1 *Prologue*

"[1]The revelation of Jesus Christ, which God gave him to show to his servants the things that must soon take place. He made it known by sending his angel to his servant John, [2]who bore witness to the Word of God and to the testimony of Jesus Christ, even to all that he saw. [3]Blessed is the one who reads aloud the words of this prophecy, and blessed are those who hear, and who keep what is written in it, for the time is near."

The Revelation to John is a book of great hope. It tells us how the world as we know it will end and be replaced with a glorious new world. Revelation is a book from Jesus, and it is about Jesus. It is about the love, fidelity, grace, and power of our Lord and Savior. It begins by telling us "the things that must soon take place" (Revelation 1:1). Revelation is communicated by an angel to John, the recorder. It brings a powerfully evocative vision of the things to come and the promise of great blessings: "Blessed is the one who reads aloud the words of this prophecy, and blessed are those who hear, and who keep what is written in it, for the time is near." (Revelation 1:3).

Revelation removes confusion, mystery, and doubt regarding God's plan for the near-term future of His creation. Jesus Christ, the King of kings, will return soon. He could come again at any moment. He will come "like a thief in the night." Jesus told us to be ready and watchful: "But concerning that day and hour, no one knows, not even the angels of heaven, nor the Son, but the Father only." (Matthew 24:36).

Revelation tells us what the return of Christ will be like and that He will return imminently. The original Greek wording is en tachei, translated as "imminently."

Greeting to the Seven Churches

"*4*John to the seven churches that are in Asia:

Grace to you and peace from him who is and who was and who is to come, and the seven spirits who are before his throne, *5*and from Jesus Christ the faithful witness, the firstborn of the dead, and the ruler of kings on earth.

To him who loves us and has freed us from our sins by his blood *6*and made us a kingdom, priests to his God and Father, to him be glory and dominion forever and ever. Amen. *7*Behold, he is coming with the clouds, and every eye will see him, even those who pierced him, and all tribes of the earth will wail on account of him. Even so. Amen.

8 "I am the Alpha and the Omega," says the Lord God, "who is and who was and who is to come, the Almighty."

The opening is followed by a greeting to seven churches in Asia. John was pivotal in establishing these churches and knew them well. The selection of seven churches is significant. Churches also existed in other locations in Roman Asia, such as Troas and Colossae. Thus, the choice of these seven—a number representing completeness—indicates that the greeting is to all churches in existence at the time. In Scripture, the number seven symbolizes the church of Christ: all churches then existing and those yet to come. It also implies perfection, and divine order.

Jesus's selection of these specific seven churches is also symbolic of persecution. The government was trying to crush the early church during a time of governmental, social, and spiritual turmoil. John wrote to reassure the church that "God was in control" and that they should remain faithful, staying their course in the face of extreme persecution, even unto Death. John stresses the eternal nature of God when he wrote, "and peace from him who is and who was and who is to come, the Almighty" (Revelation 1:8).

In Revelation 1:7, we are told that Jesus will come with the clouds of heaven and every eye shall see Him. Every person on earth will witness Christ's return. The tribes of earth will wail, dreading the judgment they are about to undergo. The unrepentant will know Christ's return as the worst day of their lives.

The church need not worry. The rapture will already have occurred; believers will be saved in the clouds of heaven. Christ is returning to judge and to work with Israel. He told us that He is the Alpha and the Omega. Being one in the triune God, Jesus has the first and last word in the history of humankind.

Christ tells us He is the beginning and the end. Believers find complete strength, peace, and salvation in Him. In Revelation 1:4, God is flanked by the Holy Spirit, referred to as the "seven Spirits," once again representing perfection, and by His Son, our Lord Jesus Christ. John focuses on Jesus the Son, who is the faithful witness, firstborn of the dead, and ruler of the "kings on earth." John emphatically tells the churches that we can believe in these revelations because they came from our Lord. As the firstborn of the dead, Christ's resurrection foretells the coming resurrection of all believers. As ruler and king on earth, Christ will soon crush His enemies and the serpent.

John MacArthur wrote: "The Book of Revelation is the ultimate action thriller. It contains drama, suspense, mystery, and horror. It tells of rebellion, unprecedented economic collapse, and the ultimate war of human history. Revelation is a book of outstanding drama and horror, but also of hope and joy. It culminates with a happy ending, as sin and Death are banished forever" (MacArthur, p. 25).

The original Greek text for this Second Coming of Christ in all His power and glory is Erchomai, or "the Coming One." This Second Coming is mentioned more than five hundred times in the Bible. As presented in the author's prior book, The Gift of Salvation, Will You Be Raised Up to the Clouds of Heaven?, Jesus will first come for believers, His church, and rapture them to the clouds of heaven. Immediately following this Pretribulational Rapture, suffering, judgment, and punishment will fall on the earth during the Great Tribulation. Christ will then return in glory to judge all sinners. The serpent will be crushed. "Those who pierced him" (Revelation 1:7) does not refer to the Crucifixion but to the unbelieving Jews who were responsible for His Death. They "and all tribes of earth will wail on account of him." (Revelation 1:7). The tribes will wail because of the judgment they will receive from Jesus Christ, Lord of all. Yet not all remaining on earth will be lost during this period. In Zechariah 12:10 and 13:1, we read of the 144,000 and their fellow Jewish followers who will be saved during the Great Tribulation and the Second Coming. Jews and

Gentiles alike will mourn. Only the repentant will be saved. Genuine repentance is required for salvation. Again, please refer to The Gift of Salvation for further discussion.

The opening of this prophecy reminds us that the Lord God is the first and the last, the Alpha and Omega. Thus, The Revelation to John is the Omega, the end of God's Sacred Word to us.

Vision of the Son of Man

[9] I, John, your brother and partner in the tribulation and the kingdom and the patient endurance that are in Jesus, was on the island called Patmos on account of the Word of God and the testimony of Jesus. [10] I was in the Spirit on the Lord's Day, and I heard behind me a loud voice like a trumpet [11] saying, "Write what you see in a book and send it to the seven churches, to Ephesus and to Smyrna and to Pergamum and to Thyatira and to Sardis and to Philadelphia and to Laodicea."

[12] Then I turned to see the voice that was speaking to me, and on turning I saw seven golden lampstands, [13] and in the midst of the lampstands one like a son of man, clothed with a long robe and with a golden sash around his chest. [14] The hairs of his head were white, like white wool, like snow. His eyes were like a flame of fire, [15] his feet were like burnished bronze, refined in a furnace, and his voice was like the roar of many waters. [16] In his right hand he held seven stars, from his mouth came a sharp two-edged sword, and his face was like the sun shining in full strength.

> [17]When I saw him, I fell at his feet as though dead. But he laid his right hand on me, saying, "Fear not, I am the first and the last, [18]the living one. I died, and behold I am alive forevermore, and I have the keys of Death and Hades. [19]Write therefore the things that you have seen, those that are and those that are to take place after this. [20]As for the mystery of the seven stars that you saw in my right hand, and the seven golden lampstands, the seven stars are the angels of the seven churches, and the seven lampstands are the seven churches.

In verse 10, John writes that when he received this profound vision, he "was in the Spirit on the Lord's Day." Being "in the Spirit" is evocative of having a transcendental or supernatural experience. While in the Spirit, John was visited by the Holy Spirit and spoken to by Jesus Christ. Such revelatory encounters with the Lord are rare in history and include Ezekiel (Ezekiel 2:2; 3:12, 14), Peter (Acts 10:9 and following), and Paul (Acts 22:17–21; 2 Corinthians 12:1). The Lord's Day, when John was in the Spirit, is not "the day of the Lord," which is the Parousia, or Second Coming of Christ. The Lord's Day is Sunday, the day on which Christ was resurrected and the day of worship for the Church.

John wrote that he was a brother and partner in the tribulation besetting the nascent church. The vision he shares brings great hope. It is the vision of an appearance by Christ, who instructs which churches were to receive the seven letters and what their content was to be.

In his vision, John sees the Son of Man in His majestic glory. Jesus, the Son of Man, was physically and spiritually present with His struggling church. The Lord's intimate knowledge of the condition and struggles of each church reveals His omniscience. He not only knew their conditions but gave commands for response and repentance. By His appearance in full power and resplendent glory, the Son of Man gave assurance that neither earthly danger nor Death would defeat His church.

God's plans were defined at the beginning of time. Daniel 7:1–14 prophesied of the Ancient of Days, dressed in clothing as white as snow, whose hair was like pure wool, and whose throne was fiery flames. He was given dominion and glory and a kingdom so that all peoples and nations could serve Him. His dominion was to last forever, never to pass away, never to be destroyed. His hair like white wool speaks of infinite and divine wisdom (Daniel 7:9). Thousands will serve Him, and ten thousand times ten thousand will stand before Him, while the court sits in judgment and the books are opened (Daniel 7:10).

John heard a loud voice like a trumpet, indicating the importance of what was to be spoken. It was the voice of the Lord. When John turned to see the voice that spoke, he saw seven golden lampstands. In the midst of the lampstands was the Son of Man, clothed in a long robe with a golden sash around His chest. This was a vision of Christ with the Holy Spirit. His feet were like burnished bronze, strong to crush opposition and evil. John heard the roar of many waters, indicating God's presence. The two-edged sword from the Lord's mouth symbolized God's Word, which sees into men's hearts and judges the wicked. The Son of Man's face shone bright like the sun. John fell at His feet when he saw the glorious presence of the Lord.

The Lord God spoke and said, "Fear not, I am the first and the last, and the living one. I died, and behold, I am alive forevermore" (Revelation 1:17–18). The Son of Man confirmed His identity and divine eternity. He who is ever-living died to redeem sinners, rose again, and lives forevermore. He tells John he must not fear Death. This is also a message to the church: do not fear Death, for Christ has conquered Death for us all.

Isaiah prophesied, "I, the Lord, the first, and with the last, I am he" (41:4) … "I have chosen you and not cast you off. Fear not, for I am with you; be not dismayed, for I am your God; I will strengthen you and help you," (41:9–10) … "Thus says the Lord, the King of Israel and his Redeemer, the Lord of hosts: 'I am the first and I am the last; besides me there is no god.'" (44:6).

1 Corinthians 15:55 gives us the indelible words of hope: "Death is swallowed up in victory. O Death, where is your victory? O Death, where is your sting?"

Jesus appeared to John to bring a message of hope and a rebuke of the shortcomings and sins of the nascent churches. Jesus was ministering to His church. He instructed John to write down the vision he was about to receive and send it to the seven churches. The order in which Jesus named the churches also had a practical purpose.

> The seven cities appear in the order that a messenger, travelling on the great circular road that linked them, would visit. After landing at Miletus, the messenger or messengers bearing the book of Revelation would have travelled north to Ephesus (the city nearest Miletus), then in a clockwise circle to Smyrna, Pergamum, Thyatira, Sardis, Philadelphia, and Laodicea. Copies of Revelation would have been distributed to each church.

(Because The Time Is Near, MacArthur, John, Moody Publishers, Chicago, 2007, p34).

Jesus tells us in Verse 20 that the seven golden lampstands, or menorahs, represent the seven churches in Asia. The seven stars are the angels of these churches. This vision and the seven churches were to bring light to the world by spreading the Gospel. Christ declares, "I died, and behold I am alive forevermore, and I have the keys of Death and Hades." (Revelation 1:18). Jesus also tells us in Matthew 5:14-15, "You are the light of the world. A city cannot be hidden. Nor do people light a lamp and put it under a basket, but on a stand, and it gives light to all in the house." John is to carry the message of Revelation to the seven churches, from where it will spread far beyond.

The glorious vision of our Lord Jesus Christ is mystical—overwhelming in its beauty and power. Christ instructs John to write down what He says and deliver it to the churches. John falls before Christ, who lays His right hand on him and says not to fear, for He is the One who, though dead, lives forevermore. Christ is the Alpha and the Omega, our "great high priest who has passed through the heavens" (Hebrews 4:14), the One from whom "we may receive mercy and find grace to help in time of need" (Hebrews 4:16). Through John, Christ brings hope, strength, and teaching of what is to come to His church.

Christ's physical appearance in this vision is formidable. The "sharp two-edged sword" from His mouth in Verse 1:16 symbolizes the Word of God. Hebrews 4:12 describes God's Word as "sharper than any two-edged sword." John, who once walked the earth with Jesus, now falls at the feet of the risen Christ, as will all believers. Moses hid his face before God. Peter fell on his face before the Lord God. (Luke 5:8).

Now John falls at the feet of the risen Lord. Being in His presence is overwhelming, yet He shows believers throughout time that they have nothing to fear before Him.

Verses 1:17-20 in the Prologue of Revelation continue this theme by telling us that His church has nothing to fear when they face the risen Lord. Verse 17 begins with John falling down as if he were dead at the feet of Jesus. John trembled in fear. This was not the first time that John fell prostrate before the Lord. Matthew 17:6 records that the apostles fell down on their faces in terror atop a high mountain when the transfiguration of Jesus occurred before their eyes. Jesus's face was shining like the sun, and His clothing was brilliant white. Moses and Elijah appeared before them and talked with Jesus. The voice of God came from a cloud and said, "This is my beloved Son, with whom I am well pleased; listen to Him." (Matthew 17:5). Jesus, the Lord God, was kind and comforting to His disciples. He touched them, telling them to have no fear.

As before, Jesus is kind and comforting to John when He appeared to John and placed his hand on John's shoulder. (Revelation 1:17 (Prologue)).

> "Fear not, I am the first and the last, and the living one. I died, and behold I am forevermore, and I have the keys to Death and Hades." (Revelation Prologue 17-18)

Jesus the Christ is the living one, the loving one, and the all-powerful one.

He explains to His church the great mysteries of His resurrection and His rule over all. He alone holds the keys to Death and Hades. Hades is Death in itself. Jesus holds all authority over who will die and who will live for eternity.

Christ alone has this authority. Thus, we will also tremble at His sight and fall before His feet in worship.

The focus soon shifts back to the present and the task at hand facing John. Jesus charges John to write down what he sees in this Revelation and take it to the seven churches. Jesus is instructing us that all Christians are responsible for sharing the truth of Christ and growing the Church.

Letters to the Seven Churches

The seven letters are addressed to the angel of each church. The letters include rebukes for shortcomings. Each church is given the command to hear and to heed all rebukes. Each also receives the promise of blessings: "To the one who conquers, the Lord will grant that they eat of the tree of life which is in the paradise of God." (Revelation 2:7).

The letters to the seven churches share common elements. Each is written to the "angel" of that church, who was perhaps the church leader, and each is tailored to the situation and vitality of that specific church. Each letter briefly describes John's vision of Christ. Five of the seven receive praise and validation. The five also receive warnings and admonitions. The problems mentioned in these letters still plague many of our churches today. Only the churches of Smyrna and Philadelphia were not admonished. Significantly, the entire Revelation to John, as he recorded it, was to be read aloud in all the churches. The Lord wanted His messages heard.

These seven letters are the first sevenfold series in Revelation, to be followed by the seven seals, seven trumpets, and seven bowls. All seven churches are commanded to hear the message in their letter and respond to its warnings. A blessing is promised to those who obey: "To the one who conquers I will grant to eat of the tree of life, which is in the paradise of God." (Revelation 2:7).

Chapter 4

Ephesus, Smyrna, Pergamum, and Thyatira

To the Church in Ephesus

²"To the angel of the church in Ephesus write: "The words of him who holds the seven stars in his right hand, who walks among the seven golden lampstands. ²"I know your works, your toil and your patient endurance, and how you cannot bear with those who are evil, but have tested those who call themselves apostles and are not, and found them to be false. ³I know you are enduring patiently and bearing up for my name's sake, and you have not grown weary. ⁴ But I have this against you, that you have abandoned the love you had at first. ⁵ Remember therefore from where you have fallen; repent, and do the works you did at first. If not, I will come to you and remove your lampstand from its place, unless you repent. ⁶ Yet this you have: you hate the works of the Nicolaitans, which I also hate. ⁷ He who has an ear, let him hear what the Spirit says to the churches. To the one who conquers I will grant to eat of the tree of life, which is in the paradise of God."

It is speculated that Jesus started the church in Ephesus. Paul officially founded it around A.D. 52. Paul preached and ministered there for about three years, and during that time, "all the residents of Asia heard the word of the Lord, both Jews and Greeks." (Acts 19:10). Timothy became its pastor in A.D. 65, followed later by John. The church's prominence is highlighted by being a recipient of four New Testament letters: *Ephesians, 1 Timothy, 2 Timothy,* and *Revelation.*

The church at Ephesus was widely known for its Christian testimony. Ephesus was a thriving city, large, prosperous, and a major commercial center of its day. It was also home to the temple of Artemis, one of the Seven Wonders of the World, dedicated to the worship of this mythological Greek pagan goddess. The Lord commended Ephesus for its many strengths: hard work, sound teaching, intolerance of evil, and perseverance. Jesus praised the church twice for its perseverance. However, He also wrote that this church had "abandoned the love you first had" (Revelation 2:4). This could mean that the church had lost its love and passion for Christ. Their works may have become rote, and their ministry mechanical. Evangelism might have declined, and their forward-looking focus weakened. Temptation abounded in this pagan city.

The Nicolaitans in Ephesus were a heretical sect, similar to Balaam. They seduced God's people into idolatry and sexual immorality. The churches that conquer will eat of the tree of life in Eden, which will appear again in the New Jerusalem. God has promised this to His church. The tree of life will be watered by the life-giving water of God's throne.

Jesus called on the church to repent and return to performing works as they did in their earlier years. God's greatest command is to make disciples. Works and service cannot replace a passionate heart. The church was admonished to return to its works and practices of its formative years. They were also called to repent. If they succeed in following these instructions, Jesus promises that they shall eat the tree of life in God's paradise. If they fail, Christ will remove their lampstand, meaning they would lose their standing as a church and be regarded and treated as an apostate state.

To the Church in Smyrna

[8] "And to the angel of the church in Smyrna write: 'The words of the first and the last, who died and came to life. [9]I know your tribulation and your poverty (but you are rich) and the slander of those who say that they are Jews and are not, but are a synagogue of Satan. [10] Do not fear what you are about to suffer. Behold, the devil is about to throw some of you into prison, that you may be tested, and for ten days you will have tribulation. Be faithful unto Death, and I will give you the crown of life. [11] He who has an ear, let him hear what the Spirit says to the churches. The one who conquers will not be hurt by the second Death."

Smyrna was located about thirty-five miles north of Ephesus. Today, the city is known as Izmir. In its day, it was a large and thriving city with a library, theaters, and stadiums. It was also the largest port on the Aegean Sea. The name *Smyrna* derives from the Hebrew word *mor*, meaning *myrrh*, an incense used in preparing the deceased for burial. Smyrna endured numerous invasions and earthquakes, yet its citizens always rebuilt. God was pleased with the steadfastness of the church in Smyrna. Jesus spoke of His own earthly sufferings, including His Death and resurrection, to show His understanding, compassion, and encouragement. He acknowledged Smyrna's suffering and poverty, yet commended them for being spiritually rich. The church in Smyrna was not cautioned or admonished by the Lord. Rather, He expressed concern because Smyrna was being severely persecuted. Business owners and proprietors were vandalized, looted, and boycotted because of their faith. Christians were imprisoned for refusing to acknowledge Caesar as lord.

Jesus encouraged the church and its martyrs, urging them not to fear the suffering they would continue to endure. He told them to remain faithful unto Death, and they would receive "the crown of life". Some biblical scholars suggest that the "crown of life" refers to a special status or standing in heaven for those who suffered deeply for their faith, even unto Death. While its exact meaning is uncertain, we do know the Lord has promised that Death has no sting. Jesus's central message to Smyrna was to endure to the end. No matter what suffering believers face, Death will have no victory over them. Christians who remain faithful until Death will know eternal life in the presence of God.

The word *tribulation*, used by Christ, translates from the Greek as "to be under pressure". The church in Smyrna was indeed under great pressure, enduring looting, financial ruin, poverty, vandalism, blasphemy, imprisonment, and even Death. Many Christian churches of that era met in Jewish synagogues. As political opposition intensified in Smyrna, Christian Jews were expelled from synagogues by Jewish instigators who assisted the Roman authorities in their persecution and imprisonment. These were the "synagogues of Satan". The "second Death" Christ spoke of was spiritual Death. For the believer, the first Death leads to eternal life. Believers will not suffer the second Death. As written in the letter to Ephesus: "To the one who conquers I will grant to eat of the tree of life, which is in the paradise of God." Thus, the church in Smyrna received only praise and encouragement from our Lord Jesus Christ.

To the Church in Pergamum

[12] "And to the angel of the church in Pergamum write: 'The words of him who has the sharp two-edged sword'.
[13] "I know where you dwell. Where Satan's throne is. Yet you hold fast my name, and you did not deny my

faith even in the days of Antipas my faithful witness, who was killed among you, where Satan dwells. [14] But I have a few things against you: you have some there who hold the teaching of Balaam, who taught Balak to put a stumbling block before the sons of Israel, so that they might eat food sacrificed to idols and practice sexual immorality. [15] So also you have some who hold the teaching of the Nicolaitans. [16] Therefore repent. If not, I will come to you soon and war against them with the sword of my mouth. [17] He who has an ear, let him hear what the Spirit says to the churches. To the one who conquers I will give some of the hidden manna, and I will give him a white stone, with a new name written on the stone that no one knows except the one who receives it.

The church at Pergamum, founded by Paul, was located in the midst of paganism. Sin and temptation abounded. The church was persecuted when it refused to worship the emperor.

Pergamum, the capital of Asia Minor, was near the ancient city of Troy and was located about one hundred miles north of Ephesus. Like Smyrna, it boasted a renowned university and a massive library. It was a medical center and a leader in the production of parchment. However, these human accomplishments marked the end of its similarity to Smyrna. Pergamum had drifted away from biblical teachings and warnings, falling back toward paganism. Numerous temples were erected to Asklepios, Dionysos, Athena, and others. The Acropolis even featured a forty-foot altar to Zeus. Perhaps this is why Christ called it the city "where Satan dwells." Yet despite the danger, believers held fast to their faith. Antipas, Christ's "faithful witness," was one such believer—and he was killed in Pergamum.

The church at Pergamum followed the teachings of Balaam, a false prophet for hire who accepted payment to curse Israel (Numbers 22–25). He advised the king that the Israelites' faith could be weakened if they intermarried with pagans from surrounding lands. This "error of Balaam" (Jude 11) encouraged God's people to intermarry with nonbelievers. To halt Israel's slide into sin, God intervened and struck down 24,000 (Numbers 25:9).

In addition, the church in Pergamum developed a pattern of compromise, adopting the teachings of the Nicolaitans. This sect was founded by Nicholas (see Acts 6:5), one of the first seven deacons in the early church. The Nicolaitans practiced sexual immorality and celebrated with pagan feasts. Claiming that they were free in Christ, they believed they were no longer obligated to abstain from fleshly desires or immorality. They also embraced Gnosticism, which taught that the physical body was evil while the spirit was not. Thus, they believed that they were free to do whatever they wished with their bodies. Yet as James reminds us: "Friendship with the world is hostility toward God" (James 4:4).

Jesus redeems us in body and soul. He called on the church in Pergamum to repent and warned that if they did not, He would come quickly to "war against them with the sword of His mouth". This sharp two-edged sword is the Word of God, which Hebrews 4:12 describes as "living and active, sharper than any two-edged sword".

Repentance is a change of mind that leads to a change in behavior. Tolerance, widely advocated through the centuries, is a pathway to heresy and sin. The church of Christ cannot tolerate evil or sin. Paul taught this in 1 Corinthians. Yet no believer is left to struggle alone. In each of the seven letters, Christ makes it clear that He is with us always. He strengthens us with His hidden manna —the Bread of Life, Christ Himself.

Christ promised that those who overcame their sin would receive manna, a white stone and a new name written on the stone. Jesus compared Himself to manna, the bread of heaven. White stones represented innocence in the courts of the day. White stones represent God's will (Exodus: 28). They also indicate valor in battle. The new name written on the stone is visible only to the recipient and could have multiple positive meanings. It is said that white stones guided high priests. In Rome, triumphant athletes were given white stones as a badge of honor.

To the Church in Thyatira

[18] "And to the angel of the church in Thyatira write: 'The words of the Son of God, who has eyes like a flame of fire, and whose feet are like the burnished bronze. [19] "I know your works, your love and faith and service and patient endurance, and that your latter works exceed the first. [20]But I have this against you, that you tolerate that woman Jezebel, who calls herself a prophetess and is teaching and seducing my servants to practice sexual immorality and to eat food sacrificed to idols. [21]I gave her time to repent, but she refuses to repent of her sexual immorality. [22]Behold, I will throw her onto a sickbed, and those who commit adultery with her I will throw into great tribulation, unless they repent of her works, [23]and I will strike her children dead. And all the churches will know that I am he who searches mind and heart, and I will give to each of you according to your works. [24]But to the rest of you in Thyatira, who do not hold this teaching, who have not learned what some call the deep things of Satan, to you I say, I do not lay on you any other burden. [25]Only hold fast what you have until I come. [26]The one who conquers and who keeps my works until the end, to him I will give authority over the nations, [27]and he will rule them with a rod of iron, as when earthen pots are broken in pieces, even as I myself have received authority from my Father. [28]And I will give him the morning star. [29]He who has an ear, let him hear what the Spirit says to the churches."

Likely founded as an outreach of Paul's work in Ephesus, the church in Thyatira tolerated sin, including idol worship, sexual immorality, and other spiritual evils. By the time this letter was written, these failings had become pervasive.

The church was located on the Roman road, about forty miles southeast of Pergamum. The city began as a military outpost established by Seleucus, who continued the mission of Alexander the Great. Thyatira was originally built to guard the road to Greece. Rome conquered the city in 190 BC and developed it into a commercial center with many guilds skilled in producing wool, fabrics, garments, metals, and other crafts. Thyatira was not a religious hub. Its primary worship was dedicated to the Greek god Apollo.

In the opening of this letter, the Son of God is described with eyes like flames of fire and feet like burnished bronze. While this imagery reflects the city's association with metalworkers, it also symbolizes Christ's power to search the mind and heart. The weakness of the church in Thyatira was its tolerance of sin.

As in the other six letters, Christ praised what was good about the church, such as their demonstrations of love for God, faith and service within the church. Christ soon turned to His concerns with the church, particularly women teachers and preachers, in particular Jezebel, a prophetess who taught idol worship and sinful ritual, including sexual immorality. Christ showed mercy, giving the "Jezebel" time to repent. She did not. Christ acted by punishing her with great physical sickness. Those church members who committed adultery with Jezebel were also punished with tribulation, and their children were stricken dead if they did not repent. Jezebel symbolizes the prostitute of Babylon, the seductress we read of in Revelation 17.

Christ encouraged the church members who had not fallen into wickedness and indulgence. Each individual's deeds and actions would determine their punishments and rewards. Christ promised those who endured with future authority

over nations. He will give them even the "morning star",
Christ Himself. This is a reference to the promise of the
saved reigning with Christ in the millennium kingdom.

Chapter 5

Sardis, Philadelphia, Laodicea

To the Church in Sardis

3"And to the angel of the church in Sardis write: 'The words of him who has the seven spirits of God and the seven stars.

"'I know your works. You have the reputation of being alive, but you are dead. 2Wake up, and strengthen what remains and is about to die, for I have not found your works complete in the sight of my God. 3Remember, then, what you received and heard. Keep it, and repent. If you will not wake up, I will come like a thief, and you will not know at what hour I will come against you. 4Yet you have still a few names in Sardis, people who have not soiled their garments, and they will walk with me in white, for they are worthy. 5 The one who conquers will be clothed thus in white garments, and I will never blot his name out of the book of life. I will confess his name before my Father and before his angels. 6He who has an ear let him hear what the Spirit says to the churches.'

Sardis was a church in trouble. John was instructed to tell the church that it was "dead." Although Sardis had a reputation for being vibrant and strong, it was merely growing in numbers and creating good impressions. Christ called the church dead. False doctrine and teaching and sinful practices killed that which might otherwise have been good about the church. The church did not internalize or live a life of faith. We read in James that faith without works is dead (James 2:17, 26). Jesus cried out to Sardis to wake up before it was too late to save themselves and their church from certain Death.

Sardis was one of the great cities of the ancient world. It was located on a plateau fifteen hundred feet above the Hermus River valley, approximately thirty miles from Thyatira. Surrounded by steep cliffs on three sides, the people of Sardis believed they were invincible to attack. It was one of the wealthiest cities in Asia, with gold mined from the Pactolus River, and was widely known for its jewelry industry. Archaeologists have discovered hundreds of instruments used in refining gold among the ruins of Sardis. The city was also a leading manufacturer of wool garments and textiles.

The Sardinians believed that their location made them secure, leading to their complacency. Accordingly, Sardis was captured by Cyrus of Persia in 549 BC and again by Antiochus in 195 BC. Later, it fell under Roman control. By the time of John's letter, the city and its structures still bore scars from these conflicts. The history of Sardis stands as a warning to be watchful, for its legacy was one of complacency.

In this letter, Christ described Himself as Almighty God, "who has the seven spirits of God and the seven stars". This description flows from the vivid vision of Christ, the Son of Man, recorded in Revelation 1:12–17. The seven stars are defined in Revelation 1:20 as the "angels of the seven churches," and the seven lampstands as the "seven churches". The number seven signifies completeness. As used in Revelation 1:12–17, this may also be a reference to Isaiah, where we read of the characteristics of the Spirit of the Lord.

"And the Spirit of the Lord shall rest upon him, the Spirit of wisdom and understanding, the Spirit of counsel and might, the Spirit of knowledge and the fear of the Lord." (Isaiah 11:2)

The "seven spirits of God" may also refer to the representation of the Holy Spirit as a lampstand with seven lamps in Zechariah 4:1–10. The Spirit of the Lord is strong, multifaceted, and represents Christ in His church.

Jesus offered no praise to the church at Sardis. Instead, He launched directly into condemnation, disregarding the church's earthly reputation for growth and vitality. Christ knew their deeds and described the church as being in a spiritual coma and dead. Their works were incomplete because they were unworthy and unacceptable in the eyes of God. Thus, Christ called the few faithful to "wake up and strengthen what remains and is about to die". Christ will come like a thief for those who do not repent. Their names shall be "blotted out of the book of life", that is, the unrepentant will know eternal spiritual Death.

As spoken by Christ, "garments" unsoiled by those few whom Christ found worthy in Sardis refer to the just. Isaiah writes, "We have all become like one who is unclean, and all our righteous deeds are like a polluted garment" (Isaiah 64:6). Jude also exhorts believers to "save others by snatching them out of the fire; to others show mercy with fear, hating even the garment stained by the flesh" (Jude 23). To the worthy, Christ promises to clothe them in white garments.

In Matthew and Mark, we read that Christ will replace earthly garments with eternal, pure white robes (Matthew 17:2; 28:3; Mark 9:3; 16:5). Those so clothed will know eternal life, for Jesus promises to "confess their names before my Father" and assures that He "will never blot their names out of the book of life."

To the Church in Philadelphia

[7]"And to the angel of the church in Philadelphia write: "The words of the holy one, the true one, who has the key of David, who opens and no one will shut, who shuts and no one opens."
[8]"I know your works. Behold, I have set before you an open door, which no one is able to shut. I know that you have but little power, and yet you have kept my word and have not denied my name. Behold, I will make those of the synagogue of Satan who says that they are Jews and are not, but lie – behold, I will make them come and bow down before your feet, and they will learn that I have loved you. [10]Because you have kept my word about patient endurance, I will keep you from the hour of trial that is coming on the whole world, to try those who swell on the earth. "I am coming soon. Hold fast what you have, so that no one may seize your crown. [12]The one who conquers, I will make him a pillar in the temple of my God. Never shall he go out of it, and I will write on him the name of my God, and the name of the city of my God, the new Jerusalem, which comes down from my God out of heaven, and my own new name. [13]He who has an ear, let him hear what the spirit says to the churches."

In stark contrast to the church at Sardis, the church at Philadelphia received only praise and encouragement from Jesus. Being human, Philadelphia was not perfect, but it was faithful. Out of the seven churches, only Philadelphia and Smyrna received unqualified praise from Christ for their faithfulness and obedience.

Philadelphia means "brotherly love," as translated from Greek. It was located about thirty miles southeast of Sardis, in what is now Turkey. Strategically positioned as a gateway to Asia, it was known for spreading the Greek language and culture. The city was built on lava fields, which proved well-suited for growing grapes. This gave rise to a significant wine trade and, according to tradition, contributed to the worship of Dionysus, the god of wine.

The letter to Philadelphia begins with the Lord Jesus Christ identifying Himself as the "Holy One." We find this title in Mark 1:24, Luke 1:35, John 6:69, and Acts 3:14. Simon Peter said to Jesus, "Lord, to whom shall we go? You have the words of eternal life, and we have believed, and have come to know, that You are the Holy One of God" (John 6:68–69).

Christ further affirms His authority by declaring that He, as "the true one," holds the key of David. In Revelation 5:5 and 22:16, David symbolizes the Messiah's role. Revelation 1:17–18 proclaims: "Fear not, I am the first and the last, and the living one. I died, and behold I am alive forevermore, and I have the keys of Death and Hades." Christ has all power.

After identifying Himself as the author of the letter to the church in Philadelphia, Jesus praised the church greatly. When He wrote that the church had "little power," He was acknowledging that, though small in number, they were strong in faith. What matters to Christ is not size but fidelity to His Word. Because of this fidelity, Christ placed an open door before them—a door that no one but Christ can shut. He praised the church for holding fast to His Word and being true followers of His teaching.

Jesus made five promises to the church at Philadelphia:

1. They would be acknowledged as true followers of Christ, and the "synagogue of Satan" would bow before their feet.
2. They would escape the tribulation to come.
3. They would soon see the Lord.
4. They would be established in God's temple.
5. They would be identified with Christ for eternity.

Their salvation was assured by their faithfulness.

In Revelation 3:10, Christ promises the church in Philadelphia: "Because you have kept my word about patient endurance, I will keep you from the hour of trial that is coming on the whole world, to try those who dwell on the earth." This promise—that Philadelphia would be spared the hour of trial, or "the tribulation"—points to their deliverance from the coming great tribulation and their being raptured into the clouds of heaven. It is a clear promise by Jesus of a pretribulational rapture of believers. For a fuller discussion, see this author's companion book *The Gift of Salvation: Will You Be Raised Up to the Clouds of Heaven?* John MacArthur affirms this view as well:

> "In keeping with the Lord's promise to spare His church from the hour of testing given in 3:10, the church will be raptured before the time of the tribulation begins." (MacArthur p.108).

This promised rapture of the church is also found in John 14:1–4, 1 Corinthians 15:51–54, and 1 Thessalonians 4:13–17. This is one of the Lord Jesus Christ's greatest promises to His church. Christ promises to keep His church from the seven years of testing, suffering, and purification of unbelievers in the coming end times. The end times are also prophesied in the Old Testament. Daniel's Seventieth Week (Daniel 9:25–27) and Jeremiah's "time of Jacob's trouble" (Jeremiah 30:7) foretell this coming period, known as the Great Tribulation.

Christ's promise to make the faithful "a pillar in the temple of my God" is a promise of eternity. His promise to "write on him the name of My God" assures a personal and everlasting relationship with our Creator. The promise of the New Jerusalem guarantees eternal life in heaven. The promise of knowing Christ's new name reveals the fullness of His Person. The church in Philadelphia will be truly and eternally blessed—and this blessing extends to all true believers.

To the Church at Laodicea

[14]"And to the angel of the church in Laodicea write: 'The words of the Amen, the faithful and true witness, the beginning of God's creation.
[15]" 'I know your works: you are neither cold nor hot. Would that you were either cold or hot! [16]So, because you are lukewarm, and neither hot nor cold, I will spit you out of my mouth. [17]For you say, I am rich, I have prospered, and I need nothing, not realizing that you are wretched, pitiable, poor, blind, and naked. [18]I counsel

you to buy from me gold refined by fire, so that you may be rich, and white garments so that you may clothe yourself and the shame of your nakedness may not be seen, and salve to anoint your eyes, so that you may see. [19]Those whom I love, I reprove and discipline, so be zealous and repent. [20]Behold, I stand at the door and knock. If anyone hears my voice and opens the door, I will come in to him and eat with him, and he with me. [21]The one who conquers, I will grant him to sit with me on my throne, as I also conquered and sat down with my Father on his throne. [22]He who has an ear, let him hear what the Spirit says to the churches.' "

Laodicea was a church in trouble. Being neither "hot nor cold" but labeled by Christ as "lukewarm" was damning. Jesus said, "I will spit you out of my mouth." Hot water is therapeutic, and cold water is refreshing. Lukewarm water, however, is repugnant. Jesus had nothing positive or hopeful to say to this church. He has wept over some churches and been angry with others, but to spit a church out of His mouth is an act of condemnation. To be lukewarm is to lack all passion and care. Indifference toward God is a rejection of God. Though He found them wretched, naked, and blind, Jesus was still willing to give this fallen church a chance.

The Laodiceans were self-assured because of their wealth. They felt they needed nothing—not even from God. Nevertheless, Christ showed patience and offered them a path to salvation. He told them to buy from Him "gold refined by fire," meaning the priceless gift of a true relationship with Him, which equates to the Lord's promise of salvation. He urged them to purchase white garments, symbolic of forgiveness of sin and saving faith, so they would no longer stand spiritually naked but be clothed in purity. The Laodiceans were blind to their own sinfulness and needed their eyes healed with salve so they could turn from darkness to light. Christ called on them to repent and listen, for He was knocking at their door. Finally, He appealed to anyone who "has an ear" to hear His message—yet tragically, there was no one.

Chapter 6

The Throne in Heaven

The Throne in Heaven

4 After this I looked, and behold, a door standing open in heaven!   And the first voice, which I had heard speaking to me like a trumpet, said "Come up here, and I will show you what must take place after this." [2]At once I was in the Spirit, and behold, a throne stood in heaven, with one seated on the throne. [3]And he who sat there had the appearance of jasper and carnelian, and around the throne was a rainbow that had the appearance of an emerald. [4]Around the throne were twenty-four thrones, and seated on the thrones were twenty-four elders, clothed in white garments, with golden crowns on their heads. [5]From the throne came flashes of lightning, and rumblings and peals of thunder, and before the throne were burning seven torches of fire, which are the seven spirits of God, [6]and before the throne there was as it were a sea of glass, like crystal.

And around the throne, on each side of the throne, are four living creatures, full of eyes in front and behind: [7]the first living creature like a lion the second living creature like an ox, the third living creature with the face of a man and the fourth living creature like an eagle in flight. [8] And the four living creatures, each of them with six wings, are full of eyes all around and within, and day and night they never cease to say,

"Holy, holy, holy, is the Lord God Almighty, who was and is and is to come!"

[9]And whenever the living creatures give glory and honor and thanks to him who is seated on the throne, who lives forever and ever,[10]the twenty-four elders fall down before him who is seated on the throne and worship him who lives forever and ever. They cast down their crowns before the throne, saying,

[11]"Worthy are you, our Lord and God, to receive glory and honor and power, for you created all things, and by your will they existed and were created."

Imagine, if you can, hearing this trumpeting voice telling you to come up here to heaven so you can see with your eyes what will take place, what heaven really is, and what it will be like to be there. This is what the Angel of God called out to John. John was immediately in the Spirit, the Holy Spirit of God, and literally saw heaven. He saw the throne of God standing before him. This was not a throne in the physical or earthly sense, but rather in a Godly sense. The Lord God Almighty and the Lamb are the temple. We will see this clearly in Revelation 21:22. The temple is not a building. It is the physical presence of God. God is eternal, unlike any physical building or temple. The Triune God is the throne of the temple, standing unshakable. The throne of God is unequaled in power. The temple is the very presence and power of our divine Father. God's rule is fixed and permanent; thus, the throne is described as standing. We do not live by chance or fortune. God controls every aspect of His creation.

Dr. Robert Jeffress, in his book Final Conquest, describes "a Place Called Heaven."

The first heaven is the atmosphere around earth (Genesis 1:6-8). It's where the birds fly, it's the air we breathe. The second heaven is outer space (Matthew 24:26). It's where the sun, moon, and stars are. The third heaven is the place where God dwells (2 Corinthians 12:2, 4). And, as we will see in Revelation 21, there will also be a fourth heaven – a future heaven that God is preparing for us right now – that will be our eternal home." (pp 76-77).

To show him "what must take place", Jesus took John up to heaven, and John was immediately in the Spirit. "At once I was in the Spirit, and behold, a throne stood in heaven, with one seated on the throne." (Revelation 4:1–2). A door to heaven was opened for John. John will be shown the impact of Christ's victory on the cross as it continues forward until the time of the new heaven and the new earth—that is, until the end of history. John's vision includes God on His throne and the slain Lamb, who will receive and open the scroll's seven seals. John sees the deliverance of God's judgment on sinners in contrast with the salvation of the saints. He sees the four living creatures and hears their unending praises of the Lord God.

The prophets foresaw God's glory in heaven in numerous visions. They were terrified by the Lord's power and glory.

"I saw the Lord sitting upon a throne, high and lifted up; and the train of his robe filled the temple. Above him stood the seraphim. Each had six wings: with two he covered his face, and with two he covered his feet, and with two he flew. And one called to another and said: "Holy, holy, holy is the Lord of hosts; the hole earth is full of his glory." (Isaiah 6:1-3).

And Micaiah said "Therefore hear the word of the Lord: I saw the Lord sitting on his throne, and all the host of heaven standing beside him on his right hand and on His left." (1 Kings 22:19).

"And above the expanse over their heads there was the likeness of a throne, in appearance like a sapphire; and seated above the likeness of a throne was a likeness with a human appearance. And upward from what had the appearance of his waist I saw as it were gleaming metal, like the appearance of fire enclosed all around. And downward from what had the appearance of his waist I saw as it were the appearance of fire, and there was brightness around him." (Ezekiel 1:26-28).

"As I looked, thrones were placed and the Ancient of Days took his seat; his clothing was white as snow, and the hair on his head like pure wool, his throne was fiery flames; its wheels were burning fire. A stream of fire issued and came out from before him; a thousand thousands served him, and thousand times ten thousand stood before him; the court sat in judgment, and the books were opened." (Daniel 7:9-10).

He who sat on the throne appeared like "jasper and carnelian, and around the throne was a rainbow that had the appearance of an emerald" (Revelation 4:3). The throne's appearance was fiery, shimmering, and splendid. Isaiah and Ezekiel received similar visions of God's glory, depicted in the colors of jasper, carnelian, emeralds, and the rainbow. Perhaps these visions are required because there were no words adequate to describe the glory, majesty, and power of God's image. Taken together, these gemstones and colors hint at the physical glory of God.

The jasper is later described by John as perfectly clear. Thus, it may be a diamond. A carnelian (translated as sardius in NKV and sardine in KJV versions, was named after the city of Sardis) is a brilliant ruby red. Brilliant red also symbolizes God's wrath and His glory. Jasper brilliantly reflects light. We learn in Genesis that the rainbow is God's covenant of grace and faithfulness with His creation. A surrounding rainbow would have its characteristic prominent green hue, suggestive of the emerald. The jasper and carnelian were the first and last stones on the breastplate worn by a high priest (Exodus 28:17–20), representing the first and last born of the twelve sons of Jacob. Some postulate that the stones represent God's covenant relationship with Israel. In addition, these stones will be the foundation stones of the New Jerusalem, God's holy city following the Great Tribulation (Revelation 21:19–20).

The twenty-four elders seated on twenty-four thrones, adorned with gold crowns and white garments, most likely represent the members of the church. The twenty-four thrones imply that they rule with Christ (Revelation 2:26–27; 3:21; 5:10; 20:4; Matthew 19:28; Luke 22:30; 1 Corinthians 6:2–3; 2 Timothy 2:12). These twenty-four will not be angels. When used in Scripture, "elders" applies to men, not to angels. The original Greek text never refers to angels. Furthermore, "white garments" designate believers, and crowns are never promised to angels in Scripture. The crown in Greek refers to the victor, a human term. Jesus promised the gold crown to believers at Smyrna if they were faithful unto Death (Rev. 2:10).

Revelation speaks to us with powerful imagery and symbolism to convey the majesty of heaven and the fulfillment of God's promises to His creation. The twenty-four thrones and the twenty-four elders might represent the orders of priests serving in the Old Testament temple (1 Chronicles 24:7–19). Perhaps it is more likely that they represent God's people of the Old Testament's twelve tribes of Israel, and the New Testament church with its twelve apostles and the twelve gates and foundations of Jerusalem (Revelation 21:12). The thrones could represent the heavenly court in Daniel 7:9–10. The lightning and thunder call back to Mount Sinai and God's appearance (Exodus 19:16). Seas of glass appear in Scripture in prophetic visions of God's throne (Exodus 24:10; Ezekiel 1:22, 26; Revelation 15:2). The floor of heaven contrasts with the ceiling of the universe, as does heavenly peace with earthly turmoil. The four living creatures reflect back to the prophetic Old Testament visions found in Isaiah 6:2–3 and Ezekiel 1:10, 18. It is said that these four creatures, who unceasingly praise God, represent the whole of creation on earth and in heaven. We will read shortly that when the Lamb breaks open the seven seals, these living creatures send out the four horsemen to bring judgment on the earth. All of these creatures and beings exclusively use their powers to offer continual praise to God for His creation and eternal perfection.

Some suggest the twenty-four are believers who were saved between Pentecost and the rapture. The twelve tribes of Israel are another suggestion. The twenty-four, in all likelihood, refer to men who have been raptured. Additionally, in Scripture we read of twenty-four officers of the sanctuary, twenty-four courses of the Levitical priests, and twenty-four divisions of singers in the temple (1 Chronicles 24:4–5). Thus, the twenty-four elders of Revelation might represent a broader group. It has been proposed that the twenty-four elders represent Israel. This supposition is not plausible because the Jews are to be converted and will live through the Tribulation. Therefore, the identity of these twenty-four elders is, in all likelihood, the raptured church, all of whom will be standing before the throne in heaven. The hearts and minds of all believers should not waver. We will be with the Lord. We are not to be troubled.

> "Let not your hearts be troubled. Believe in God; believe also in me. In my Father's house are many rooms. If it were not so, would I have told you that I go to prepare a place for you? And if I go and prepare a place for you, I will come again and take you to myself that where I am you may be also. And you know the way to where I am going." (John: 14:1-4).

We read of the rapture of the church in Philadelphia in Revelation 3:10. God's promise to spare His believers from the suffering to come in the tribulation is repeatedly made in 1 Thessalonians 1:10; 5:9; 4:13–18, 2 Peter 2:5–9, 1 Corinthians 15:51–58, Matthew 24:36–44, John 14:3, and Revelation 1:7; 3:10.

In Revelation 6–18, we find the tribulation in full fury, with no mention of the church. The church will have been spared and already raptured to heaven before the time of trials begins. The tribulation will be the time of salvation for the Jews and condemnation of unbelievers.

Revelation 4:5 vividly foretells the coming "flashes of lightning and rumbles and peals of thunder" indicative of the presence of God. In Ezekiel 1:4–14, "stormy winds and great clouds", bright fire, and flashes of lightning indicate the presence and approach of God. Exodus 19:16 records the approach of God at Mount Sinai, announced by flashes of lightning, thunder, and a trumpet blast so intense that the people trembled. The coming judgment by Jesus the Christ at the time of the Great Tribulation will also be accompanied by lightning and thunder. Scripture tells us repeatedly that cosmic power, demonstrated in intense lightning and thunder, will accompany the Lord in times of judgment.

The Lord's coming war against sin and His time of judgment will be all-powerful and terrifying for those judged to be among the depraved. John saw seven torches, or lamps of fire, burning in front of the throne, which are identified as "the seven spirits of God" (Revelation 5:5). The Old

Testament identifies torches as weapons of war (see Judges 7:16, 20; Nahum 2:3–4). This vision that John sees in Revelation suggests that Christ is ready for war. It will be Christ's war against sin and the depravity of man.

We are next given another glimpse of heaven. A sea of "glass, like crystal" covered the space in front of and before the throne. This glass is like a shimmering and clear pavement. Moses, Aaron, Nadab, Abihu, and seventy elders of Israel saw "under God's feet in heaven a pavement like sapphire stone, like the very heaven for clearness" (Exodus 24:10).

There were four creatures with eyes surrounding their heads, in the front and at the back. Each creature had six wings. These "living creatures" are described as a lion, an ox, a man, and an eagle in flight. They are symbolic of all of God's creation and its greatness. Just as believers will praise God for eternity in heaven day and night, the four creatures praised the holiness of God, and "never ceased to say":

"Holy, holy, holy, is the Lord God Almighty, who was and is and is to come!". (Revelation 4:8).

In song, the creatures simultaneously signify and praise the omnipotence of God. A repetition of three times indicates superlative praise. These four creatures represent all of God's creation in their worship of our Creator. God's power, recorded throughout Scripture, was perhaps most visibly displayed in the destructions of Sodom and Gomorrah, Pharaoh's armies, and many of the most powerful leaders of history, such as Nebuchadnezzar. It will be God who delivers the terror of the Great Tribulation at the End of Times. These creatures cry out "He who was and who is and who is to come" (Revelation 4:8), for they know that God is eternal and all-powerful.

The twenty-four elders then fall prostrate in worship of the Lord, and the four creatures sing praise to the Lord. The elders throw their gold crowns before the throne and cry out "Worthy are you, Lord and God…you created all things…" (Revelation 4:11). The elders represent the church. In God's time, we, the church, will join the twenty-four elders and spend eternity praising Him.

Chapter 7

The Scroll and the Lamb

The Scroll and the Lamb

5Then I saw in the right hand of him who was seated on the throne a scroll written within and on the back, sealed with seven seals. [2]And I saw a mighty angel proclaiming with a loud voice, "Who is worthy to open the scroll and break its seals?" [3]And no one in heaven or on earth or under the earth was able to open the scroll or to look into it, [4]and I began to weep loudly because no one was found worthy to open the scroll or look into it. [5]And one of the elders said to me, "Weep no more; behold, the Lion of the tribe of Judah, the Root of David, has conquered, so that he can open the scroll and its seven seals."
[6]And between the throne and the four living creatures and among the elders I saw a Lamb standing, as though it had been slain, with seven horns and with seven eyes, which are the seven spirits of God sent out into all the earth. [7]And he went and took the scroll from the right hand of him who was seated on the throne. [8]And when he had taken the scroll, the four living creatures and the twenty-four elders fell down before the Lamb, each holding a harp, and golden bowls full of incense, which are the prayers of the saints. [9]And they sang a new song, saying,

"Worthy are you to take the scroll
and to open its seals.
  for you were slain, and by your blood
you ransomed people for God

from every tribe and language and
people and nation." (Revelation 5:9)
[10]and you have made them a kingdom
and priests to our God,
and they shall reign on the earth."

[11]Then I looked, and I heard around the throne and the living creatures and the elders the voice of many angels, numbering myriads of myriads and thousands of thousands, saying with a loud voice,

[12] "Worthy is the Lamb who was slain,
to receive power and wealth and wisdom and might
and honor and glory and blessing!

[13]And I heard every creature in heaven and on earth and under the earth and in the sea, and all that is in them, saying,

 "To him who sits on the throne and to the Lamb
be blessing and honor and glory and might forever and
ever!"

[14] And the four living creatures said, "Amen!" and the elders fell down and worshiped."

The precious blood of the Lamb, Jesus the Christ, our Lord and Savior, redeemed us.

"…knowing that you were ransomed from the futile ways inherited from your forefathers, not with perishable things such as silver or gold, but with the precious blood of Christ, like that of a lamb without blemish or spot. He was known form the foundation of the world but was made manifest in the last times for the sake of you who though him are believers in God, who raised him from the dead and gave him glory, so that your faith and hope are in God." (1 Peter 1:18-21).

John saw Christ holding a scroll sealed with seven seals in His right hand. An angel cried out, "Who is worthy to open the scroll and break its seals?" (Revelation 5:2). Only Christ the Lamb, the Lion of the Tribe of Judah, who conquered Death, was able to open the scroll. Only the Lamb is worthy. Seven is the number of perfection and of the triune God. This scroll is from the Lord God, and none but the triune God can break the seals. It was also a requirement under Roman law that wills be sealed seven times. The scroll is the book of redemption. It is further revealed in Revelation 6–8. Many have tried to speculatively answer the question of the contents of the scroll. One of the best-proposed answers is by Dr. Robert Jeffress of the First Baptist Church, Dallas, Texas;

> I believe that it is a scroll that shows how the paradise God created was forfeited to Satan. The Scroll also contains events that must take place for this universe once and for all to be redeemed and delivered to its rightful owner, God the Father. The scroll in the Father's hand was so important that it could not be opened by just anyone, even the strongest of the angels.

The Lord God tells us that it is the Rood of David, the Lamb that may open the sacred scroll:

> "Weep no more; behold, the Lion of the Tribe of Judah, the Root of David, has conquered, so that he can open the scroll and its seven seals." (Revelation 5:5)

Scripture introduces the Lion of the Tribe of Judah in the blessing by Jacob on the tribe of Judah, as recorded in Genesis 49:8–10. A strong and fierce ruler was foretold. Yet John saw a Lamb, not a Lion.

The Lamb is not known for its strength or ferocity. Furthermore, in the original Greek, the word "arnion" is used, which translates to "little lamb".

The Root of David is also named. It originates in Isaiah 11:1, 10 and recurs in Matthew 1 and Luke 3. Jesus descended from David's royal bloodline from the lineage of both Mary and Joseph. As a descendant of King David, Jesus is also the rightful and powerful King.

Scrolls were not typically inscribed on both sides. Being of leather or papyrus, they were difficult to inscribe, and one side could be rough. It is interesting, however, that Roman law required contracts, wills, and deeds to be written in detail on one side and summarized or labeled on the outside of a scroll. This sacred scroll might symbolize God's covenant with His creation—perhaps suggestive of a will, or a covenant with creation that would pour out curses if man broke it, or perhaps the contents reveal God's purposes for history. No one was worthy or had sufficient authority to open this scroll except for the Lamb. This discloses both Jesus's royal descendancy from the Root of David and how Jesus conquered Death.

When Jesus the Lamb receives the scroll, the four living creatures and the twenty-four elders sing a new song celebrating the redemption of the Lamb. The elders fall down prostrate to worship the Lamb, praising His divinity. They praise the Lion that was slain as the Lamb, thereby ransoming Himself to save the multitudes of humanity with the sacrifice of His blood. We next read that a kingdom of priests to our God will reign on earth. The choir explodes in growth and power. Every creature of the earth and the seas is praising the Lamb in song. The four living creatures cried "Amen", and the elders fell down in worship of the Lamb.

The gifts of Christ to us are far too great for any human measure. First, Jesus submitted to God in all things. Jesus released His rights as God Himself, as an equal member of the triune God, and became fully human, sacrificing Himself so that we might live. Christ became fully man and died on the cross so that we might have eternal life with Him. This is the very same Christ who had seven horns and seven eyes, which are the seven spirits sent out to all the earth (Revelation 5:6). Seven is the number of perfection and completion. The seven horns represent the omnipotence of Christ. He had all power and all strength. The seven eyes represent His divine wisdom. The seven Spirits are the Holy Spirit. John saw a Lamb. It was the divine Lamb, the Son of God and the triune God. Christ is that very Lamb who takes away the sin of the world in John 1:29. In Revelation, Christ is referred to as the Lamb of God thirty-one times, more than in any other book of Scripture.

> "Worthy are you who take the scroll
>   and to open its seals,
> for you were slain, and by your blood
>   you ransomed people for God
> from every tribe and language and
>   people and nation." (Revelation 5:9)

The massive chorus of angels present in this vision numbered myriads of myriads and thousands of thousands, which calculates in contemporary arithmetic as approximately two hundred million angels. We cannot even imagine a chorus of two hundred million vocalists. The heavens were fully present. God's home, heaven, is magnificent beyond our human ability to comprehend. John was understandably overcome with awe, praise, and wonder. Furthermore, the angels praised the Lamb for His seven attributes of perfection: power, riches, wisdom, might, honor, glory, and blessing. The Lamb is almighty.

The chorus of praise was heard by all creatures in heaven, under the earth, and in the sea. Who are those under the earth? They are the non-Christians who will go to hades upon their Death. Thus, it might be that those in hades will see Christ for who He is and praise Him. Tragically, they will be too late for salvation.

Chapter 8

The Seven Seals

The Seven Seals

6Now I watched when the Lamb opened one of the seven seals, and I heard one of the four living creatures say with a voice like thunder, "Come!" [2]And I looked, and behold, a white horse! And its rider had a bow, and a crown was given to him, and he came out conquering, and to conquer.

[3]When he opened the second seal, I heard the second living creature say, "Come!" [4]And out came another horse, bright red. Its rider was permitted to take peace from the earth, so that the people should slay one another, and he was given a great sword.

[5]When he opened the third seal, I heard the third living creature say, "Come!" And I looked, and behold, a black horse! And its rider had a pair of scales in his hand. [6]And I heard what seemed to be a voice in the midst of the four living creatures, saying, "A quart of wheat for a denarius, and three quarts of barley for a denarius, and do not harm the oil and the wine!"

[7]When he opened the fourth seal, I heard the voice of the fourth living creature say, "Come!" [8]And I looked, and behold, a pale horse! And its rider's name was Death, and Hades followed him. And they were given authority over a fourth of the earth, to kill with sword and with famine and with pestilence and by wild beasts of the earth.

[9]When he opened the fifth seal, I saw under the altar the souls of those who had been slain for the word of God and for the witness they had borne. [10]They cried out with a loud voice, "O Sovereign Lord, holy and true,

how long before you will judge and avenge our blood on those who dwell on the earth?" [11]Then they were each given a white robe and told to rest a little longer until the number of their fellow servants and their brothers should be complete, who were to be killed as they themselves had been.

[12]When he opened the sixth seal, I looked, and behold, there was a great earthquake, and the sun became black as a sackcloth, the full moon became like blood, [13]and the stars of the sky fell to the earth as the fig tree sheds its winter fruit when shaken by a gale. [14]The sky vanished like a scroll that is being rolled up, and every mountain and island was removed from its place. [15]Then the kings of the earth and the great ones and the generals and the rich and the powerful, and everyone, slave and free, hid themselves in the caves and among the rocks of the mountains, [16]calling to the mountains and rocks, "Fall on us and hide us from the face of him who is seated on the throne and from the wrath of the Lamb, [17]for the great day of their wrath has come, and who can stand?"

Revelation 6:1–17 reveals the beginning of the Great Tribulation. Jesus told His disciples what the end of times would be like. The opening of the first four seals is symbolic of Jesus Christ the Lamb's power to use wicked humans to deliver God's punishment on the persecutors of His faithful. In Matthew's Gospel, we read in the Olivet Discourse:

"Jesus left the temple and was going away, when his disciples came to point out to him the buildings of the temple. But he answered them, "You see all these, do you not? Truly, I say to you there will not be left here one stone upon another that will not be thrown down." As he sat on the Mount of Olives, the disciples came to him privately, saying, "Tell us, when will these things be, and what will be the sign of your coming and of the end of the age?" And Jesus answered them, "See that no one leads you astray. For many will come in my name, saying 'I am the Christ,' and they will lead many astray. And you will hear of wars and rumors of wars. See that you are not alarmed, for this must take place, but the end is not yet. For nation will rise against nation, and kingdom against kingdom, and there will be famines and earthquakes in various places. All these are but the beginning of the birth pains. And then they will deliver you up to tribulation and put you to Death, and you will be hated by all nations for my name's sake. And then many will fall away and betray one another and hate one another. And many false prophets will arise and lead many astray. And because lawlessness will be increased, the love of many will grow cold. But the one who endures to the end will be saved. And this gospel of the kingdom will be proclaimed throughout the whole world as a testimony to all nations, and then the end will come." (Matthew 24:1-14).

Christ was clear that destruction, Death, and tribulation of many forms will occur at the end of times. These will be the times of "Abomination and Desolation" written of in the Old Testament. Christ told His disciples to be ready for what will come to pass. Christ has warned His church of the approach of a horrific end of times.

"So when you see the abomination of desolation spoked of by the prophet Daniel, standing in the holy place (let the reader understand), then let those who are in Judea flee to the mountains. Let the one who is on the housetop not go down to take what is in his house…For then there will be a great tribulation, such as has not been from the beginning of the world until now, no, and never will be." (Matthew 24:15-22).

In Revelation 6, John was taken up, or raptured, to heaven. He was to see all that is to come at God's final judgment. John sees the seven seals opened by the Lamb, and they will release the wrath of God on creation. The Lamb shall bring the enemies of the Lord to justice.

When the first of the seven seals was broken by the Lamb, a white horse, ridden by the first of the Four Horsemen of the Apocalypse, appeared. Roman soldiers rode white horses in victory parades. In this vision, the rider of the white horse is the Antichrist. The rider of the white horse comes to conquer with his bow. The Bible tells us that after the church is raptured, the Antichrist will emerge as the leader of the world. He will make a false peace with Israel so that he can gain the people's trust, only to kill the Jews during the second three and one-half years of the tribulation. "And he shall make a strong covenant with many for one week… And on the wing of abominations shall come one who makes desolate, until the decreed end is poured out on the desolator." (Daniel 9:27). The same warning is given in the New Testament: "For you yourselves are fully aware that the day of the Lord will come like a thief in the night. While people are saying "There is peace and security," then sudden destruction will come upon them as labor pains come upon a pregnant woman, and they will not escape." (1 Thessalonians 5:2–3). Death and destruction will fall upon the people just when they are not heeding the Word and are believing peace and safety is theirs.

The colors of the horses align with Zechariah 1:8–10 and 6:1–8, which foretell emissaries sent by God to patrol the earth.

> I saw in the night, and behold, a man riding on a red horse! He was standing among myrtle trees in the glen, and behind him were red sorrel, and white horses. Then I said, "What are these my lord?" The angel who talked with me said to me, "I will show you what they are." So the man who was standing among the myrtle trees answered, "These are they whom the Lord has sent to patrol the earth." Zechariah 1:8-10

> Again I lifted my eyes and saw, and behold, four chariots came out from between two mountains. And the mountains were mountains of bronze. The first chariot had red horses, the second black, horses, the third white horses, and the fourth chariot dappled horses – all of them strong. Then I answered and said to the angel who talked with me, "What are these, my lord? And the angel answered and said to me, "These are going out to the four winds of heaven, after presenting themselves before the Lord of all the earth. The chariot with the black horses goes toward the north country, the white ones go after them, and the dappled ones go toward the south country." When the strong horses came out, they were impatient to go and patrol the earth. And he said, "Go, patrol the earth." So they patrolled the earth. Then he cried to me, "Behold, those who go toward the north country have set my spirit at rest in the north country."

The visions in Revelation 6 foretell how the Lamb will bring His enemies to justice as the seven seals are broken. The seal, trumpet, and bowl judgments are grouped into four judgments of the earth and three cosmic judgments. The breaking of the final three seals will unleash the most horrific cosmic judgments, demonstrating God's wrath, including His final judgment at the end of time. The Lamb will direct forces that inflict Death by the sword, famine, pestilence, and wild beasts.

As the Lamb breaks open each of the first four seals, a horse and rider appear. A white horse, whose rider wore a crown and carried a bow, appeared first. He came to conquer. This rider is symbolic of political and military leaders and their disabling force on society, leading to wars and Death.

When the Lamb opened the second seal, the second of the creatures exclaimed, "Come". A second horse came out, bright red in color—the color of blood. The rider of the red horse held a great sword with double sharp edges. This greatly armed rider foretells bloodshed and Death. The horse's brilliant red color especially suggests war and bloodshed. He was charged to end peace on earth and usher in the murderous behavior of the people on earth.

Paul wrote of the coming of the Antichrist and the terror of the "man of lawlessness," whom the Lord had been restraining. The opening of the second seal will remove the restraints on Satan, the lawless one. These events will introduce times of great bloodshed and wars. Great destruction is to come. "For nation will rise against nation, and kingdom against kingdom." (Matthew 24:7).

Upon the opening of the third seal of judgment, a black horse came at the call of the third living creature. The black horse will bring a great famine. Scripture associates famine with the color black: "Our skin was black like an oven because of the terrible famine." (Lamentations 5:10). The rider of the black horse was holding scales so he could measure grains and their escalating prices. John heard a voice coming from the middle of the four living creatures. This voice could well be the voice of God. The voice was calling out the prices of wheat and barley, principal food sources of the times. The prices were eight-fold the normal prices, indicating food shortages and famine. Yet luxury items of wine and oil were not affected, thus famine among the poor coincided with plenty for the wealthy. This occurred under Domitian's reign circa A.D. 92, when there was a grain shortage, but the vineyards were maintained for the wealthy, whereas the grain fields were cut down, impacting the poor.

At the opening of the fourth seal, again a voice called out, "Come!" A pale horse came forth, its rider being named Death. A pale or ashen color suggests Death. Hades followed Death. Hades and Death were given all authority over one-fourth of the earth and were to kill all its inhabitants with sword, famine, pestilence, and wild beasts. Hades is the god of the underworld in Greek mythology and was associated with great earthly wealth.

*One fourth of the earth's current population today would be billions of people.

Never before will the earth have seen such massive Death and destruction. Jesus described this as a time "great tribulation, such has not been from the beginning of the world until now, no, and never will be.

"For there will be great tribulation, such as has not been from the beginning of the world until now, no, and never will be. And if those days had not been cut short no human being would be saved. But for the sake of the elect those days will be cut short. Then if anyone says to you, 'look, here is the Christ!' or 'There he is!' do not believe it. For false christs and false prophets will arise and perform great signs and wonders, so as to lead astray, if possible, even the elect. See, I have told you beforehand. So, if they say to you, 'Look, he is in the wilderness, do not go out. If they say, 'Look, he is in the inner rooms, do not believe it. For as the lightning comes from the east and shines as far as the west, so will be the coming of the Son of Man. Wherever the corpse is, there the vultures will gather." Matthew 24:21-28. See 21-1-25

"And if those days had not been cut short, no human being would be saved. But for the sake of the elect, those days will be cut short." (Matthew 24:21–27).

The opening of the fifth seal reveals images of the martyrs. It marks the midpoint of the tribulation. The second half of the tribulation will see the unleashed fury of God. The martyrs are those who will be slain for their testimony to Jesus the Christ, our Lord and Savior. They cried out to the

Lord God for mercy, and judgment and retribution for their blood. The Lord gave each a white robe of purity. He told them to rest for a while, for more believers are to be slain. The white robe is symbolic of God's gift of virtue and justice. This is assurance from Christ that after the rapture of His church of believers, those who are converted and become believers during the Great Tribulation will also be saved.

When the sixth seal was opened, a great earthquake shook the earth, the sun turned black as a sackcloth, and the moon turned as red as blood. The Book of Joel prophesied: "The sun shall turn to darkness, and the moon to blood, before the great and awesome day of the Lord comes." (Joel 2:31). Stars fell from the sky to the earth. The sky was split apart and vanished, being rolled up like a scroll. Mountains and islands were removed from their places. Kings and the rich and powerful hid in fear in caves and among rocks, as did all on the earth. The outpouring of God's wrath and power was terrifying. It appeared as the end of times and is the second half, the most terrifying part of the Great Tribulation. There was not one who could withstand the wrath of God, and humankind tried to hide their faces from Christ, whom they could see seated on the throne of judgment. Rather than pray to God for mercy and forgiveness, they called out to the rocks to crush them. Death appeared easier than standing before Christ to face judgment with a repentant heart.

John MacArthur vividly describes the Antichrist in a way that suggests he is among us now:

> "As the head of a Western confederacy, Antichrist will initially portray himself as a champion of peace. He will even appear to bring peace to the troubled Middle East. He will make a treaty with Israel, posing as their protector and defender. Soon afterwards, however, his desire for dominance will provoke rebellion. Antichrist's attempts to crush his enemies will last throughout the remainder of the tribulation. Finally, when Jesus Christ returns, Antichrist will be cast into the lake of fire forever (20:10)."
> (MacArthur p. 129)

Those who wait for the second coming will be too late. Christ will come to judge and to condemn. The sinners' only hope is to come to Christ before it is too late. Christ warns us and warned all His disciples that the time is near. He will come soon, very soon. "Now is the day of salvation."
(2 Corinthians 6:2).

Chapter 9

The 144,000 of Israel Sealed

The 144,000 of Israel Sealed

7After this I saw four angels standing at the four corners of the earth, holding back the four winds of the earth, that no wind might blow down on earth or sea or against any tree. [2]Then I saw another angel ascending from the rising of the sun, with the seal of the living God, and he called with a loud voice to the four angels who had been given power to harm earth and sea,[3]saying, "Do not harm the earth or the sea or the trees, until we have sealed the servants of our God on their foreheads." [4]And I heard the number of the sealed, 144,000, sealed from every tribe of the sons of Israel:

[5]12,000 from the tribe of Judah were sealed
12,000 from the tribe of Reuben,
12,000 from the tribe of Gad,
12,000 from the tribe of Asher,
12,000 from the tribe of Naphtali,
12,000 from the tribe of Manasseh,
12,000 from the tribe of Simeon,
12,000 from the tribe of Levi,
12,000 from the tribe of Issachar,
12,000 from the tribe of Zebulun,
12,000 from the tribe of Joseph,
12,000 from the tribe of Benjamin were sealed.

The angel who will ascend from the rising of the sun in the east comes from the quadrant associated in Scripture with divine help. This angel comes to seal, or protect, the Israelites by giving each the seal of Almighty God. Every Christian has this protective seal of God. Paul wrote in Ephesians 1:13-14 that having "believed in him, (you were) sealed with the promise of the Holy Spirit, who is the guarantee of our inheritance". God has removed sin's power over His believers. Notably, there are no Gentiles among the 144,000. This is because the church of believers will have already been raptured. The believers will already be in heaven.

The 144,000 are to be God's witnesses and workers among the nations. They will be a unique group of Jewish believers who will be chosen to proclaim the gospel. Every tribe of Israel is to be included in the 144,000. God plans that Israel will bring His light to the Gentiles, as revealed in the gospels.

> "You are the light of the world. A city set on a hill cannot be hidden.[15]Nor do people light a lamp and put it under a basket, but on a stand, and it gives light to all in the house. [16]In the same way, let your light shine before others, so that they may see your good works and give glory to your Father who is in heaven." (Matthew: 5:14-16).

Genesis 12:1-3 states that the Israelites are to be a blessing to all the earth. "They, like Saul (the apostle Paul), will be set apart to be God's witnesses to the Gentiles." (J. Dwight

Pentecost). They will be a great nation and evangelists to the world.

The 144,000 will not include all Jewish believers at the time. They will be a select group. Those who insist that the 144,000 will be all Jewish believers, the full church, are incorrect.

> "Despite the plain and unambiguous declaration of the text that the one hundred and forty-four thousand who are to be sealed will come from every tribe of the sons of Israel, many persist in identifying them as the church. But the identification of Israel with the church in those passages is tenuous and disputed. The fact is that "no clear-cut example of the church being called 'Israel' exists in the New Testament or in ancient church writings until A.D. 160…This fact is crippling to any attempt to identify Israel as the church in Revelation 7:4. The term Israel must be interpreted in accordance with its normal biblical usage as a reference to the physical descendants of Abraham, Isaac, and Jacob." (Because The Time Is Near, Moody Publishers, Chicago2007, John MacArthur, p. 142).

The 144,000, selected by God, will form a great and powerful missionary force. Again, the 144,000 will be commissioned by Christ for great works. Jesus told His disciples that the kingdom gospel is to be taught to the world before His Second Coming. As sinners are saved and follow Christ, God takes away the power of sin. God gives His Holy Spirit to the pardoned sinner. The Holy Spirit is with the saved, who one day will be raised to eternal life in heaven. The Holy Spirit is the seal for all those who will be saved.

However, the seal on the 144,000 is different. It is the "seal of the living God" (Revelation 7:2) and of the twelve tribes of Israel, Jacob's descendants. God will save the 144,000 from His wrath. God called Israel to be His witness to all nations.

"But now thus says the Lord, he who created you, O Jacob, he who formed you, O Israel: Fear not, for I have redeemed you; I have called you by name and you are mine.

2When you pass through the waters, I will be with you; and through the rivers, they shall not overwhelm you; when you walk through fire you shall not be burned, and the flame shall not consume you.

3For I am the Lord your God, the Holy One of Israel, your Savior. I give Egypt as your ransom, Cush and Seba in exchange for you.

4Because you are precious in my eyes and honored, and I love you, I give men in return for you, peoples in exchange for your life.

5Fear not, for I am with you; I will bring your offspring from the east, and from the west I will gather you.

6I will say to the north, Give up, and to the south, Do not withhold; bring my sons from afar and my daughters from the end of the earth,

7everyone who is called by my name, whom I created for my glory, whom I formed and made,

8Bring out the people who are blind, yet have eyes, who are deaf yet have ears!

9All the nations gather together, and the peoples assemble. Who among them can declare this, and show us the former things? Let them bring their witnesses to prove them right, and let them hear and say, It is true. [10]You are my witnesses, declares the Lord, and my servants whom I have chosen, that you may know and believe me and understand that I am he. Before me no god was formed, nor shall there be any after me. [11]I, I am the Lord, and besides me there is no savior. [12]I declared and saved and proclaimed, when there was no strange god among you; and you are my witnesses, declares the Lord, and I am God." (Isaiah 43:1-12).

God's plan is that Israel will be His witness, and the 144,000 sealed from the twelve tribes of Israel are to be light to the Jews and to the Gentiles who will hear. We see this declaration throughout God's written Word. During the coming Great Tribulation, the 144,000 sealed from the twelve tribes are sealed from harm so that they may evangelize. They will bring people to Christ, saving them from the lake of fire.

"You are the light of the world. A city set on a hill cannot be hidden. Nor do people light a lamp and put it under a basket, but on a stand, and it gives light to all on the house. In the same way, let your light shine before others, so that they may see your good works and give glory to your Father who is in Heaven." (Matthew 5:14-16).

While the Great Tribulation will bring suffering unlike the world has ever seen, there will be God's army of 144,000 sealed evangelists, who will save souls, particularly in regard to the Jews. At this very time, the multitude of raptured believers will be praising God in heaven. The suffering, in particular the seven seals, trumpets, and bowls, will be applied only to sinners during the Great Tribulation. The number of 144,000 Jewish believers who are sealed are protected and saved to do God's work in evangelizing. The number symbolically represents the twelve tribes of Israel. We will read more about them in Revelation 14:1-4. These 144,000 answer the question of "Who can stand?" against the earthquake and winds in Revelation 6:12-17. Being sealed, they are protected by God and His angels. The seal of the living God evokes an official's or royal's wax seal by signet ring. It is an official stamp or mark, but it is the mark of the Lord. It is the seal of the Lamb of God, also noted in Revelation 14:1. It proclaims the power of God and will crush the mark of the beast.

A Great Multitude from Every Nation

[9] After this I looked, and behold, a great multitude that no one could number, from every nation, from all tribes and peoples and languages, standing before the throne and before the Lamb, clothed in white robes, with palm branches in their hands, [10]and crying out with a loud voice, "Salvation belongs to our God who sits on the throne and to the Lamb!"   [11]And all the angels were standing around the throne and around the elders and the four living creatures, and they fell on their faces before the throne and worshiped God, [12]saying, "Amen! Blessing and glory and wisdom and thanksgiving and honor and power and might be to our God forever and

ever! Amen." [13]Then one of the elders addressed me, saying, "Who are these, clothed in white robes, and from where have they come?" [14]I said to him, "Sir, you know." And he said to me, "These are the ones coming out of the great tribulation. They have washed their robes and made them white in the blood of the Lamb.

[15]"Therefore they are before the throne of God,
and serve him day and night in his temple;
and he who sits on the throne will shelter them with his presence
They shall hunger no more, neither thirst anymore;
the sun shall not strike them
nor shall any scorching heat.
For the Lamb in the midst of the throne will be their shepherd,
and he will guide them to springs of living water,
and God will wipe away every tear from their eyes."

The great multitude in heaven standing before the throne and before Jesus Christ the Lamb will be the tribulation saints. God will rescue them from the great wrath. They will be those saved during the tribulation. The pretribulation saints were raptured before the tribulation. The tribulation saints will be both the Jewish evangelists who persevered and those whom the evangelists saved to Christ during the tribulation. People from all walks of life will come to Christ, but many will not and will be condemned to eternal suffering.

The white robes that clothe the tribulation saints in heaven will signify that they were cleansed and purified of their sins.

Their robes will be washed in the blood of the Lamb. Washing garments in blood was essential to spiritual cleansing, as recorded in Hebrews 10:4. We also read in Zechariah of the adornment with pure vestments after being cleansed of sin. Only the blood of Christ will blot out the sin of man.

> "And the angel said to those who were standing before him, "Remove the filthy garments from him." And to him he said, "Behold, I have taken your iniquity away from you, and I will clothe you with pure vestments". And I said, "let them put a clean turban on his head". So they put a clean turban on his head and clothed him with garments. And the angel of the Lord was standing by." (Zechariah 3:4-5).

The tribulation saints will serve God continuously and for eternity. The Lord's promise will be fulfilled: "I will never leave you nor forsake you." (Hebrews 13:5). The sinner who comes to Christ during the Great Tribulation will be saved, but there is no such chance if Death comes first.

> Indeed, under the law almost everything is purified with blood, and without the shedding of blood there is no forgiveness of sins." (Hebrews 9:22).

> After this I heard what seemed to be the loud voice of a great multitude in heaven, crying out, "Hallelujah! Salvation and glory and power belong to our god, for his judgements are true and just; for he has judged the great prostitute who corrupted the earth with her immorality,

and has avenged on her the blood of his servants."
(Revelation 19:1-2).

Let there be no doubt. Christ our Lord and Savior shed His Blood on the Cross so that His believers would be saved. Christ sacrificed once for all who come to Him.

Chapter 10

The Seventh Seal and the Golden Censer

The Seventh Seal and the Golden Censer

8When the Lamb opened the seventh seal, there was silence in heaven for about half an hour. [2]Then I saw the seven angels who stand before God, and seven trumpets were given to them. [3]And another angel came and stood at the altar with a golden censer, and he was given much incense to offer with the prayers of all the saints on the golden altar before the throne, [4]and the smoke of the incense, with the prayers of the saints, rose before God from the hand of the angel. [5]Then the angel took the censer and filled it with fire from the altar and threw it on the earth, and there were peals of thunder, rumblings, flashes of lightning, and an earthquake.

Revelation 8 reports the breaking of the seventh seal and advances the unfolding of the Great Tribulation. The Tribulation will be terrifying for the living. Almighty God's power and wrath will be unrestrained, and He will crush sin. There will be unprecedented destruction. Human terror will reach levels never before known. All this begins to viscerally unfold in Revelation 8.

Man has fallen far into sin and despair compared to the blessed days in the Garden of Eden. In Genesis 1:3-25, God pronounced all of His creation to be "good", and human beings "very good". However, Eve and Adam succumbed to Satan's temptation. Satan lured Eve with the temptation of knowledge and power. His false promise to Eve was that she would become "God-like", if she only ate the forbidden fruit. Eve ate the fruit and brought down Adam with her. God's punishment was severe. Woman would know pain in childbirth from that moment forward. Man and woman would sweat in their labors and were no longer immortal. They were created out of dust, and God commanded, "to dust you shall return" (Genesis 3:19). God cursed the ground we walk on, and man knows great suffering as the result of original sin. Yet the suffering that humankind has known is nothing like the suffering to come during the Great Tribulation. However, believers need not fear. Christ will come for His church of believers before the Tribulation begins.

Paul teaches us in Romans:

> For the creation was subjected to futility, not willingly, but because of him who subjected it, in hope [21]that the creation itself will be set free from its bondage to corruption and obtain freedom of the glory of the children of God. [22]For we know that the whole creation has been groaning together in the pains of childbirth until now. And not only the creation, but we ourselves, who have the first fruits of the Spirit, groan inwardly as we wait eagerly for adoption as sons, the redemption of our bodies. [24]For in this hope we are saved.

Now hope that is seen is not hope. For who hopes for what he sees? [25]But if we hope for what we do not see, we wait for it with patience." (Romans 8:20-25).

John was shown what is coming soon. Revelation begins by telling us, "The Revelation of Jesus Christ, which God gave him to show to his servants the things that must soon take place." (Revelation: Prologue 1). Salvation will come to the faithful. The worthy of God's creation will be set free from the bondage of sin and suffering. God's creation will soon be adopted as sons and experience the redemption of their bodies. For now, believers are called to wait with patience.

After Jesus the Lamb opens the seventh seal in Revelation 8:1, there was total silence in heaven for one half hour. The angels' silence anticipates the judgment of the Lord, which will be swiftly delivered. Man has never before known anything like the coming Great Tribulation. All those present with the Lamb in heaven witnessed His opening of the seventh seal. Heaven's saints were overwhelmed by the day of the Lord that will come, and were thus in their state of silence for thirty minutes. We read in the Old Testament, "Be silent before God! For the day of the Lord is near." (Zephaniah 1:7), and, "Be silent, all flesh, before the Lord, for he has roused himself from his holy dwelling." (Zechariah 2:13).

In Revelation 4:8, the four living creatures continuously prayed out loud, "Holy, holy, holy is the Lord God, the Almighty, who was and who is and who is to come!" The

Lord is about to come in fury. Revelation 8:1 foretells the unfolding of God's full wrath, which will be poured out on sin.

Seven is the number of perfection. Seven angels appear in Revelation 8:2. Paul saw them standing before God. They were given seven trumpets. An eighth angel then appeared. This angel is seen standing before the inner altar of the temple, holding a censer of gold.

It is recorded throughout the Old Testament that the Jews used trumpets to call, gather, celebrate, and launch wars. Trumpeters would lead armies in battle. Trumpets were part of holy day celebrations. Trumpets took down the wall of Jerico. Jesus told us that trumpets will announce the second coming of the Messiah.

> "Then will appear in heaven the sign of the Son of Man, and then all the tribes of the earth will mourn, and they will see the Son of Man coming on the clouds of heaven with power and great glory. And he will send out his angels with a loud trumpet call, and they will gather his elect from the four winds, from one end of heaven to the other." (Matthew 24:31).

Saint Paul tells us in 1 Thessalonians, the great rapture passage, that the sound of trumpets will announce the coming of Christ for His Church before the Great Tribulation begins.

For the Lord himself will descend from the heaven with a cry of command, with the voice of an archangel, and with the sound of the trumpet of God. And the dead in Christ will rise first. [17] Then we who are alive, who are left, will be caught up in the clouds to meet the Lord in the air, and so we will always be with the Lord. Therefore encourage one another with these words. (1 Thessalonians 16-18).

The gold censer held by the eighth angel is a vessel in which burning coal is carried by the high priest in the inner altar area. It was used to throw the burning coals onto incense that had been placed on the golden altar. This ritual would take place once each year on the Day of Atonement. The fragrant smoke would rise from the burning incense that it might be pleasing to God. The censer was historically linked with prayers of the priests. God's people were present as this ritual was performed.

There were two altars in a temple. The first was the outer altar in a courtyard where animal sacrifices were made. Because of the blood that was spilled in animal sacrifices, this first altar was separated from the inner altar, the most holy place where incense was burned in sacrifice. The pure clouds of sweet-smelling smoke from the incense rose up to the Lord God and pleased Him.

In Exodus 30:3-6, we read that the altar for burning incense was to be made of gold. This altar was to be in front of the mercy seat, before the throne, and near where God dwelt. Isaiah prophesied of the seraphim flying with burning coal in his hands. In Ezekiel 10:2, the prophet describes the altar before the throne and the casting of burning coals over the city. Interestingly, in John's vision of heaven, there is only one altar that served all functions. Perhaps that is because, unlike the earthly temple, there is no animal sacrifice to soil the altar in heaven.

The Lord does not have infinite patience with rebellious behavior and sin. God's wrath will soon be meted out, after giving sinners time for repentance. God also hears the pleas of His people who suffer in their earthly life. In God's time, fiery devastation will descend on the defiant sinners and the wicked of humanity.

The seven angels standing before God stood ready with seven trumpets. "Another angel came forward and stood at the altar holding a golden censer. He was given much incense to offer with the prayers of all the saints on the golden altar before the throne." (Revelation 8:3). The prayers of the saints and smoke from the burning incense rose up and pleased God. The rising prayers and smoke of the incense imply that the judgments that will soon follow are an answer to the saints' prayers. The rising smoke is also symbolic of the suffering church.

The angel then filled the censer he was holding with fire from the golden altar and threw it down upon the earth, "and there were peals of thunder, rumblings, flashes of lightning, and an earthquake." (Revelation 8:5). The power and majesty of God's holy throne was on display. This punishing judgment shows restraint. A succession of devastating judgments will follow. The Great Tribulation will ultimately come into its full force and fury, ending in the day of final judgment.

The seven angels with the seven trumpets act next.

The Seven Trumpets

[6]Now the seven angels who had the seven trumpets prepared to blow them.

[7]The first angel blew his trumpet, and there followed hail and fire, mixed with blood, and these were thrown upon the earth. And a third of the earth was burned up, and a third of the trees were burned up, and all green grass was burned up.

[8]The second angel blew his trumpet, and something like a great mountain, burning with fire, was thrown into the sea, and a third of the sea became blood. [9] A third of the living creatures in the sea died, and a third of the ships were destroyed.

[10]The third angel blew his trumpet, and a great star fell from heaven, blazing like a torch, and it fell on a third of the rivers and upon the springs of water. [11]The name of the star was Wormwood. A third of the waters became wormwood, and many people died from the water, because it had been made bitter.

[12]The fourth angel blew his trumpet and a third of the sun was struck, and a third of the moon, and a third of the stars, so that a third of their light might be darkened, and a third of the day might be kept from shining, and likewise a third of the night.

[13]Then I looked, and I heard an eagle crying with a loud voice as it flew directly overhead, "Woe, woe, woe to those who dwell on the earth, at the blasts of the other trumpets that the three angels are about to blow!"

When the first angel blew his trumpet, hail mixed with fire and with blood was thrown down on the earth. One-third of the earth was destroyed in flames. Although destruction of one-third of the earth will be cataclysmic, it demonstrates Almighty God's restraint. It exemplifies the wrath that will follow if His warnings are ignored. The trees and grass were all burned up, reminiscent of the seventh plague of Egypt. (Exodus 9:24). The second angel blew his trumpet, and a fireball the size of a great mountain was thrown into the sea, and one-third of the oceans were turned into blood. One-third of the life in the sea was killed, and the ships and ocean vessels destroyed. The second trumpet concludes with the sea turning to blood, reminiscent of Exodus 7:20–21, where it is recorded that when Moses struck the Nile River with his staff, its water was turned to blood. The third angel blew his trumpet, and a huge star, perhaps a giant meteor, fell from the skies, on fire and blazing like a massive torch. It fell into the rivers, and one-third of the rivers and potable waters were turned into wormwood. Many died from the spoiled waters. The fourth angel blew his trumpet, and one-third of the sun, the moon, and the stars were blackened, blocking the light from shining. Such was the ninth plague on Egypt that caused complete darkness for three days, found in Exodus 10:21–23.

hen John hears an eagle cry loudly, saying, "Woe, woe, woe to those who dwell on the earth, at the blasts of the other trumpets that the three angels are about to blow!" (Revelation 8:13). God's wrath is terrifying, but it will not fall on His church. The eagle's cry warns the wicked that time is running out.

These trumpet blasts, plagues, and cataclysmic disasters will be experienced by unrepentant sinners. Believers, those already saved and members of Christ's church, will have been raptured before the Great Tribulation begins. This is the time for delinquent repentance and God's punishment of the unrepentant wicked. Some theologians suggest that God's judgments will manifest in nuclear or chemical warfare. It seems not worth much time to reflect on this. It might be helpful, however, for those who struggle with God's Word to think of His wrath through a contemporary lens.

But how are we to know this? It is told to us in Scripture, the sacred Word of God. Christ is coming to rapture, or transport up to heaven, His church of believers. The saved will leave the false promises, vapid glories, and devastating sins of earth to live in the clouds of the sky with Jesus the Christ for eternity. Christ's church will be removed from the earth before the cleansing and judgment of sinners begins. Believers, living and dead, will be raptured to the clouds of heaven. Believers will be spared the coming of terrifying purification by the Lord God.

The seven angels will soon blow their seven trumpets, announcing the next expressions of wrath. The seven-year

Great Tribulation will be launched by the first angel's blast of his trumpet.

Many struggle to "interpret" Scripture. For many, Scripture is too intense to accept as it is written. We must understand that the Lord God will not tolerate unrepentant sin and Satanic evil without limit. Scripture lays bare our sinful natures. Also, many lack true faith and are unable to bring themselves to believe the Word of God and that sin will ultimately be punished.

The Word transcends our humanness. The Word is all-powerful and true. Humankind will never be able to fully understand or predict God. We just need to obey and believe God. His Word is the only path to salvation. The Word is given to us so that we may know and trust in the path to eternal salvation.

In Revelation 8:7, the "bowl judgments" begin, along with the seven years of God's wrath being poured out on the earth. The focus shifts from the risen Christ and His angels in heaven back to earth.

> "The first angel blew his trumpet, and there followed hail and fire, mixed with blood, and these were thrown upon the earth." (Revelation 8:7).

Many today have forgotten history. God helps us greatly by recording history in the Bible. Ancient times were scarred with plagues, famines, and wars. Little has changed over the centuries. Ten plagues that devastated Egypt preceded the exodus of Israel. Pharaoh's arrogant rejection of God led to his punishment after he said, "Who is the Lord that I should obey His voice and let Israel go?" (Exodus 5:2). God answered Pharaoh's arrogant question with earthquakes and virtually every other imaginable type of human suffering. All suffering is the consequence of the fall of man in the Garden of Eden.

It is written in Scripture that during the seven-year Great Tribulation, people will be rebellious towards the Lord, refusing to seek Him and ask for His forgiveness. Instead, sinners will refuse to submit to God's will and His teaching. This will be in spite of the land, sea, and rivers being destroyed, one-third of the trees on earth—which total three trillion (Nature Magazine)—being destroyed by fire, all the earth's green grass being destroyed by fire, and a tremendous earthquake. With trees, grass, and infrastructure destroyed by a massive earthquake, many additional calamities will likely ensue, such as crime, floods, crop failures, mudslides, lava flows, and starvation. There will be devastating loss to all life forms on earth.

Some theologians and preachers speculate on the exact details and extent of the destruction, predicting giant meteors, comets, and other calamities. These are misguided theories of men, in efforts to explain and interpret for a deeper human understanding. God did not give us His Word to confuse us or cause us to think deeply and analytically to understand. We only need to read Holy Scripture and accept it as written. Scripture is the divine Word of God. The Lord gave us His Word so that we might understand and, especially, that we would believe. Saint Peter instructed, "But by the same word the heavens and earth that now exist are stored up for fire, being kept until the day of judgment and destruction of the ungodly" (2 Peter 3:7). The nations should be far more concerned with what is to come soon from all the power of Almighty God, of which all have been warned, than contemporary political and social distractions.

God's wrath is a "dirty subject" for many of today's preachers. God is a wrathful God. However, He is first a loving, merciful, forgiving, and kind God. His wrath is real, but believers will not know it. Unrepentant sinners will.

The wrath of God is repeatedly revealed in Scripture—in Genesis, Exodus, Job, Psalms, Ezekiel, Joel, and other Books. The Lord clearly wants us to understand His wrathful side, but even more so wants us to live in His love.

The Revelation to John, the final book of the Bible, is to be taken seriously. Real fire will descend on the earth. Death, destruction, and devastation will occur. There will be no rebuilding until Christ returns to earth at the end of seven horrific years of tribulation and the punishment of sin. At the end of the seven years, the Parousia, or Second Coming, will usher in peace on earth. Jesus the Christ will be victorious in battle with Satan and will judge all sinners, casting them into hell. Following this will be a new earth and one thousand years of peace on earth with Christ and His believers. All suffering will be replaced with God's love and glory and eternal peace for all believers.

Returning to the sacred text, we read of a second angel whose attention is focused on the sea. He blew his trumpet, and a massive fiery object was cast into the sea. This object will have the appearance of a mountain consumed in the flames of fire. It will cause one-third of the sea to become blood, and one-third of all living creatures of the sea to die, and one-third of the ships of the sea to be destroyed, perhaps by catastrophic waves. The sinfulness of man will cause God to destroy fully one-third of the world's seas, which originally were given to man as a blessing.

In A.D. 2013, a sixty-five-foot-wide meteor exploded over Russia, releasing thirty times the destructive power of the atomic bomb dropped on Hiroshima. A sixty-five-foot meteor is a fraction of the size of a mountain-like object. Imagine the power of a mountain in flames that will crash into the ocean. Massive waves will result. The foretold destruction of one-third of all sea vessels and sea creatures will be devastating. Food sources, land masses, global transportation, commerce, and trade will be irreparably damaged. It is estimated that one million or more life forms live in the oceans. Loss of oceanic animal life will be catastrophic. Contemporary concerns over global warming and climate change are mere distractions compared to the biblical prophecy in Revelation that we are told will soon come to pass.

The next event to occur is the third angel blowing his trumpet: "A great star fell from heaven, blazing like a torch, and it fell on a third of the rivers and on the springs of water. The name of the star is Wormwood." (Revelation 8:10–11).

This star fell on the waterways, turning them into wormwood, resulting in a multitude of Deaths from the poisoned water. Wormwood is mentioned several times in the Old Testament and was associated with poison and Death (Exodus 15:22–25, Deuteronomy 28:18, Proverbs 5:4, Jeremiah 9:15, 23:15, Lamentations 3:15). In Revelation, the wormwood destroys one-third of the earth's fresh waters.

The fourth angel blew his trumpet, "and a third of the sun was struck, and a third of the moon, and a third of the stars, so that a third of their light might be darkened, and a third of the day might be kept from shining, and likewise a third of the night." (Revelation 8:12). Much of the world will be in darkness. Darkness was a judgment seen throughout the Old Testament (Ezekiel 32:7–8, Isaiah 13:9–10, Joel 2:10, 31, 3:15, Amos 8:9). Darkness causes cold temperatures, crop failures, fear, crime of all kinds, and many other hardships.

John heard the cry of an eagle that flew directly over him, crying out of the woe that is coming from three angels who are about to blow their trumpets. God always warns—and often warns again and again—of the coming danger of His wrath. Man typically does not heed. John then hears a warning cry out: "Woe, woe, woe to those who dwell on the earth, at the blasts of the other trumpets that the three angels are about to blow!" (Revelation 8:13). Stating a warning three times raises the warning to the highest level of alarm. This is a warning cry that things on earth are about to become much worse.

Chapter 11

The Fifth Angel

9 And the fifth angel blew his trumpet, and I saw a star fallen from heaven to earth, and he was given the key to the shaft of the bottomless pit. [2]He opened the shaft of the bottomless pit, and from the shaft rose smoke like the smoke of a great furnace, and the sun and the air were darkened with the smoke from the shaft. [3]Then from the smoke came locusts on the earth, and they were given power like the power of scorpions of the earth. [4]They were told not to harm the grass of the earth or any green plant or any tree, but only those people who do not have the seal of God on their foreheads. [5]They were allowed to torment them for five months, but not to kill them, and their torment was like the torment of a scorpion when it stings someone [6]And in those days people will seek Death and will not find it. They will long to die, but Death will flee from them.

[7]In appearance the locusts were like horses prepared for battle: on their heads were what looked like crowns of gold; their faces were like human faces, [8]their hair like women's hair, and their teeth like lions' teeth; [9]they had breastplates like breastplates of iron, and the noise of their wings was like the noise of many chariots with horses rushing into battle. [10]They have tails and stings like scorpions, and their power to hurt people for five months is in their tails. [11]They have as king over them the angel of the bottomless pit. His name in Hebrew is Abaddon, and in Greek he is called Apollyon.

[12]The first woe has passed; behold two woes are still to come.

[13]Then the sixth angel blew his trumpet, and I heard a voice from the four horns of the golden altar before God,

[14]saying to the sixth angel who had the trumpet, "Release the four angels who are bound at the great river Euphrates." [15]So the four angels, who had been prepared for the hour, the day, the month, and the year, were released to kill a third of all mankind. [16]The number of mounted troops was twice ten thousand times ten thousand; I heard their number. [17]And this is how I saw the horses in my vision and those who rode them, they wore breastplates the color of fire and of sapphire and of sulfur, and the heads of the horses were like lions' heads, and fire and smoke and sulfur came out of their mouths. [18]By these three plagues a third of mankind was killed, by the fire and smoke and sulfur coming out of their mouths. [19]For the power of the horses is in their mouths and in their tails, for their tails are like serpents with heads, and by means of them they would.
[20]The rest of mankind, who were not killed by these plagues, did not repent of the works of their hands nor give up worshiping demons and idols of gold and silver and bronze and stone and wood, which cannot see or hear or walk, [21]nor did they repent of their murders or their sorceries or their sexual immorality or their thefts.

The first four angels blew their trumpets in judgment that focused wrath upon the earth. The next three angels sound their trumpets in judgment of the non-believers. At the sound of the fifth trumpet, John saw a star fallen from heaven to earth, and he, the fallen star, was given a key to "the shaft of the bottomless pit."

The star is an angelic being. The stars and angels of heaven are the sons of God: "When the morning stars sang together and all the sons of God shouted for joy" (Job 38:7). This statement speaks of the court of the saints and angels that surround God's throne, as presented in the first chapter of the Book of Job. To have fallen from heaven is wording used in Scripture for fallen angels, demonic beings, and the foot soldiers of Satan. The bottomless pit is the holding place for demons. Isaiah wrote of the demon: "How art thou fallen from heaven, O Lucifer, son of the morning! How art thou cut down to the ground, which didst weaken the nations!" (Isaiah 14:12).

The inhabitants of the bottomless pit were already judged and were being held captive until their final judgment by Christ, which will result in their eternal punishment of being cast into the lake of fire. Verse 2 begins by telling us that this fallen angel opens the bottomless pit, and a great smoke arose so that the sun and air were darkened. The prophet Joel warned: "The sun shall be turned to darkness, and the moon to blood, before the great and awesome day of the Lord comes." (Joel 2:31). Revelation is continuous throughout the Bible.

The wicked who will die before Christ returns to earth to make His final judgment during the time of His Parousia will be temporarily held in the bottomless pit. It will be a horrible experience to live through and a preview of their ultimate eternal life in the lake of fire.

"But the children of the kingdom shall be cast out into outer darkness: there shall be weeping and gnashing of the teeth." (Mattew 8:12).

"And in Hades, being in torment, he lifted up his eyes and saw Abraham far off, and Lazarus at his side. And he called out, Father Abraham, have mercy on me, and send Lazarus to dip the end of his finger in the water and cool my tongue, for I am in anguish in this flame." (Luke 16:23-24).

"In hell all laws are overturned – there is no thought of family or country, of ties, of relationships. The damned howl and scream at one another, their torture and rage intensified by the presence of beings tortured and raging like themselves. All sense of humanity is forgotten. The howls of suffering sinners fill the remotest corners of hell. The mouths of the damned are full of blasphemies against God and of hatred for their fellow sufferers and of curses against those souls which were their accomplices in sin. They turn upon those accomplices and upbraid them and curse them. But they are helpless and hopeless: it is too late now for repentance." ("A Portrait of the Artist as a Young Man", James Joyce, New York, Everyman's Library, 1991, pp. 151-152).

"And in those days people will seek Death and will not find it. They will long to die, but Death will flee from them." (Revelation 9:6).

A swarm of locusts will come out of the smoke from the bottomless pit. It will be unlike anything known to humankind. This locust swarm will be the continued unfolding of God's punishment, which has included locust swarms throughout history.

Locusts were among the plagues of Egypt.

> "The Locusts came up over all the land of Egypt and settled over the whole country of Egypt, such a dense swarm of locusts as had never been before, nor ever will be again. They covered the face of the whole land, so that the land was darkened, and they ate all the plants in the land and all the fruit trees that the hail had left. Not a green thing remined, neither tree nor plant of the field, through all the land of Egypt." (Exodus 10:14-15).

The greatest locust swarm known to man thus far occurred in 1889, when a locust swarm over the Red Sea covered 2,000 square miles. This coming swarm will cover the entire earth, creating agony and punishment for five months. The Lord gave them instructions to terrify and torment the people, but not to kill them. Those who seek Death during this time shall not find it. The locusts were to attack only the people, stinging them like scorpions, but not to eat the grass or any green thing on the earth.

The locusts' leader is the "angel of the abyss"; thus, the locusts are demonic, and their leader is guided by Satan. The locusts are ferocious, intelligent, powerful, and swift. Their appearance reinforces their demonic nature. It will be terrifying, with gold crowns, the faces of men, hair like a woman's, teeth like lion's fangs, and breastplates of iron. Their tails are like those of scorpions and have great power. They come to do battle. They will march and attack like soldiers under the command of the angel of the abyss, whose name in Hebrew (Abaddon) and in Greek (Apollyon) is translated "Destroyer." Their crowns are symbolic of victory. This horrific event will occur during the time of the Great Tribulation. It will be a time without precedent or equal in its display of God's wrath pouring out on unrepentant sinners. God will cleanse the earth of sinners. The day of judgment has begun.

Some take the position that the angel "fallen from heaven" is Satan; however, Scripture does not support this position. This is clear according to Ephesians 6:12 and Revelation 20:1–3. The Lord has a plan for the fallen star, who is a satanic spiritual force, an agent of Satan.

> "For we do not wrestle against flesh and blood, but against the rulers, against the authorities, against the cosmic powers over this present darkness, against the spiritual forces of evil in the heavenly places." (Ephesians 6:12).

> Then I saw an angel coming down from heaven, holding in his hand the key to the bottomless pit and a great chain. And he seized the dragon, that ancient serpent, who is the devil and Satan, and bound him for a thousand years, and threw him into the pit, and shut it and sealed it over him, so that he might not deceive the nations any longer, until the thousand years were ended. After that he must be released for a little while." (Revelation 20:1-3).

The Locusts released from the bottomless pit will be given a precise mission. Recall that they will be instructed not to hurt the grass or the earth or anything that is green. Only men who have the seal of God on their foreheads will be spared. Thus, all the unbelievers who do not have the seal of God will be unprotected. No one is to be killed. Death would bring relief from the suffering they will endure. Rather, unbelievers will suffer the power and wrath of the Lord. God alone will decide when each person is to die. The people without the saving seal of God will be tormented and will suffer greatly for the five-month season of the locusts. Many think that the locusts represent the military forces we know of today, while others still believe they will be locusts that have been described to us in imagery. What matters most in this ongoing discussion is that we understand that God's destructive army is coming and will be in the form He chooses.

The sounding of the sixth trumpet by the sixth angel will release the second woe, a demonic army. John literally heard a voice coming from the golden altar that sits before God. John MacArthur suggests that this voice could be the voice of Jesus the Christ (MacArthur, p. 165). God called for the four angels who were "bound at the great river Euphrates" (Revelation 9:13) to be released so that they could kill one-third of mankind. Holy angels are never bound. Only demonic angels are bound, and God has a plan for these four whom He ordered unbound.

> These four demonic angels have been kept in chains, ready for this specific purpose. They will be released at the appropriate time during the great tribulation to fulfill God's purpose for them (Revelation 9:15). In other words, their release would occur on the very hour of the very day of the very month of the very year when the alarm on God's clock sounds." (Final Conquest, Rober Jeffers, Ph.D., Pathway to Victory, 2020, p. 148).

John tells us there would be two hundred million armed horsemen ready to execute God's command. "The number of mounted troops was twice ten thousand times ten thousand; I heard their number." (Revelation 9:16). This will be a huge demonic army, perhaps composed of fallen angels. The horses have great power and demonic appearances, with heads like lions, and fire, smoke, and brimstone spewing from their mouths. The horses' "tails are like serpents with heads, and by means of these they wound" (Revelation 9:19). They will kill by trapping human armies to war.

Twenty-five percent of the world's population had already died during the fourth seal judgment; now one-third of the survivors will be killed. This comes in response to the prayers of the saints, offered as incense at the golden altar (Revelation 8:4–5). Fully one-half of the earth's population of eight billion people will soon be killed. Such destruction by a massive army will require logistics that suggest the army is also supernatural. The soldiers will wear breastplates of fire, hyacinth, and brimstone. The colors of each are red, dark blue, and yellow, which are the colors of hell as we will read later in Revelation. This calls back to God's punishment of Sodom with destruction.

> "Then the Lord rained down on Sodom and Gomorrah sulfur and fire from the Lord out of heaven. And he overthrew those cities, and all the valley, and all the inhabitants of the cities, and what grew on the ground." (Genesis 19:24-25).)

Many think that the locusts represent the military forces we know of today, while others still believe they will be locusts that have been described to us in imagery.

Dr. Robert Jeffress presents a strong hypothesis that brings this prophecy into today.

> "I believe John was seeing a demonically inspired human army using modern weapons of warfare. Now let's use a little sanctified imagination. If the apostle John, in the first century, was trying to describe weapons of modern war such as tanks, helicopters, missile launchers, and whatever new weapons may exist in the future, what kind of language would he use? This is what I believe John was attempting to do in verses 17-19. He is describing a real war with real forces at work." (Jeffress p. 150)

Despite the suffering, destruction, and massive Death caused by the fifth and sixth trumpets, the survivors will still not repent. There will be no repentance because of their total depravity. They will continue, even increase, their practices of idol worship, demon worship, and immorality. Torture from the locusts and mass Death will only seem to push sinners deeper into sin and rebellion. To this day, Paul's hopeful expression to Timothy has not occurred.

> "Perhaps God may grant them repentance leading to the knowledge of the truth, and they may come to their senses and escape from the snare of the devil, having been held up captive by him to do his will." (2 Timothy 2:25-26).

The message to the church in Revelation 9 is well stated by John MacArthur:

> "Under the influence of the massive demonic forces, the world will descend into a morass of false religion, murder, sexual perversion, and crime unparalleled in human history. It is sobering to realize that the Lord will one day come "to execute judgement upon all" (Jude 15). In light of that coming judgement, it is the responsibility of all believers to faithfully proclaim the gospel to unbelievers, thereby "Snatching them out of the fire" (Jude 23)". (MacArthur, p. 169).

The time is closer at hand than many believers may think, let alone the nonbelievers who will continue to live in denial and sin.

Chapter 12

The Angel and the Little Scroll

The Angel and the Little Scroll

10 [1]Then I saw another mighty angel coming down from heaven, wrapped in a cloud, with a rainbow over his head, and his face was like the sun, and his legs like pillars of fire. [2]He had a little scroll open in his hand. And he set his right foot on the sea, and his left foot on the land, [3]and called out with a loud voice, like a lion roaring. When he called out, the seven thunders sounded. [4] And when the seven thunders had sounded, I was about to write, but I heard a voice from heaven saying, "Seal up what the seven thunders have said, and do not write it down." [5]And the angel whom I saw standing on the sea and on the land raised his right hand to heaven[6] and swore by him who lives forever and ever, who created heaven and what is in it, the earth and what is in it, and the sea and what is it, that there would be no more delay, [7]but that in the days of the trumpet call to be sounded by the seventh angel, the mystery of God would be fulfilled, just as he announced to his servants the prophets.

[8] Then the voice that I had heard from heaven spoke to me again, saying, "Go, take the scroll that is open in the hand of the angel who is standing on the sea and on the land." [9]So I went to the angel and told him to give me the little scroll. And he said to me. "Take and eat it; it will make your stomach bitter, but in your mouth, it will be sweet as honey." [10]And I took the little scroll from the hand of the angel and ate it. It was as sweet as honey in my mouth, but when I had eaten it my stomach was made bitter. [11]And I was told, "You must again

prophesy about many peoples and nations and languages and kings."

Revelation 10 is a change of pace leading up to the final trumpet blast. It is a brief pause in the display of God's wrath crushing the nonbelievers and the unfaithful.

John's vision has concluded. He again finds himself firmly on the earth, listening to voices from heaven. An angel comes to him again. This angel is mighty and spectacular, "wrapped in a cloud, with a rainbow over his head" (Revelation 10:1). Some incorrectly suggest that, being so spectacular in appearance, this angel must be Jesus Christ. Christ is not an angel. Christ is the triune God and is never referred to as an angel. However, this is indeed a very powerful angel, giant in size, with a loud and roaring voice. The rainbow is God's visible promise to creation that He will never again flood the earth. An angel adorned with a rainbow suggests that this angel is sent by God with His message of faithfulness to His people. He will protect believers in the coming trials and cleansing. God is faithful to believers, and they will not suffer.

The angel is huge in stature, with one foot on the sea, the second on land, and his right hand raised to heaven. The angel thus unites the three components of God's created order. The angel holds a little scroll, or book, in his hand. The scroll was open, but we do not know what was written in it. The scroll being open means that Jesus the Lamb had opened it. This is a message to John from Jesus.

John heard the angel call out in the roaring voice of a lion, and seven thunders sounded. The thunders were messages to John. A voice from heaven commanded John not to write down in his book what the thunders said. Perhaps John was told of the punishment of the wicked during the tribulation, and it was too terrifying to be written down. The angel swore by "Him who lives forever and ever and created heaven" (Revelation 10:6) that what he would speak of was God's truth. In the days ahead, the seventh angel will sound a trumpet, and the mystery of God will be fulfilled (Revelation 10:7). God's plan is that the sound of the seventh trumpet will unite heaven and earth under Christ's rule: "According to his purpose, which he set forth in Christ as a plan for the fullness of time, to unite all things in him, things in heaven and things on earth" (Ephesians 1:10).

John was then told by the voice from heaven to take the scroll from the angel and eat it. This message conveyed in the scroll held by the angel was for John alone.

> "And he said to me, "Son of man, eat whatever you find here. Eat this scroll, and go, speak to the house of Israel." So I opened my mouth, and he gave me this scroll to eat. And he said to me, "Son of man, feed your belly with this scroll that I give you and fill your stomach with it." Then I ate is, and it was in my mouth as sweet as honey." Moreover, he said to me, "Son of man, all my words that I shall speak to you receive in your heart, and hear with your ears." (Exekiel 3:3, 10)

John is to embody the Word before he speaks it to the people. The Word is sweet; the rejection and sin of the nonbelievers are bitter. There is much sadness and tragedy in life on earth. John tells us:

> And I took the little scroll from the hand of the angel and ate it. It was sweet as honey in my mouth, but when I had eaten it my stomach was made bitter." (Revelation 10:10)

John received the Word of God and absorbed it bodily by eating the scroll. The revelations contained in the scroll could be of future times, beyond the Great Tribulation. Certainly, the wrath of God, which will soon be meted out during the Great Tribulation, will turn the stomach bitter. It is very clear there will be great suffering by the nonbelievers and sinners during these seven years. There will also be sweetness for the saved. For His reasons, the Lord wanted only John to know what was written in the scroll. This passage is also a call back to Daniel 12:4, when Daniel was told to "shut up the words and seal the book, until the time of the end." Similar examples of internalizing and absorbing the Word of God are found in Psalm 19:10; Jeremiah 15:16; Ezekiel 2:9, 3:1–3; and 2 Corinthians 12:14.

Eating the scroll, as John did, is a message for all believers. We are to internalize God's Word and His teaching. We all know how to do this in our quiet times—in prayer, meditation, in our churches, and in reading our Bible.

Chapter 13

The Two Witnesses

The Two Witnesses

11Then I was given a measuring rod like a staff, and I was told, "Rise and measure the temple of God and the altar and those who worship there, [2]but do not measure the court outside the temple; leave that out, for it is given over to the nations, and they will trample the holy city for forty-two months. [3]And I will grant authority to my two witnesses, that they will prophesy for 1,260 days, clothed in sackcloth."

[4]These are the two olive trees and the two lampstands that stand before the Lord of the earth. [5]And if anyone would harm them, fire pours from their mouth and consumes their foes. If anyone would harm them this is how he is doomed to be killed. [6]They have the power to shut the sky, that no rain may fall during the days of their prophesying, and they have power over the waters to turn them into blood and to strike the earth with every kind of plague as often as they desire. [7]And when they have finished their testimony, the beast that rises from the bottomless pit will make war on them and conquer them and kill them, [8]and their dead bodies will lie in the street of the city that symbolically is called Sodom and Egypt, where their Lord was crucified. [9]For three and a half days some from the peoples and tribes and languages and nations will gaze at their dead bodies and refuse to let them be placed in a tomb, [10]and those who dwell on the earth will rejoice over them and make merry and exchange presents, because these two prophets had been a torment to those who dwell on the earth. [11]But after three and a half days a breath of life

from God entered them, and they stood up on their feet, and great fear fell on those who saw them. [12]They had heard a loud voice from heaven saying to them, Come up here!" And they went up to heaven in a cloud, and their enemies watched them. [13]And at that hour there was a great earthquake, and a tenth of the city fell. Seven thousand people were killed in the earthquake, and the rest were terrified and gave glory to the God of heaven.
[14]The second woe has passed; behold, the third woe is soon to come.

By the time the Great Tribulation begins, the Jews will have built a new temple in Jerusalem. Jewish worship will be flourishing in the temple. At the midway point in the Great Tribulation, after the first forty-two months or 1,260 days, the Antichrist will take "his seat in the temple of God, proclaiming himself to be God" (2 Thessalonians 2:4).

God speaks to John in Revelation 11:1 and tells him to measure the temple of God and its altar, and those who worship there. The original Greek word for "temple" meant the place of holiness—the "holy of holies"—where God was. The altar likely referred to the bronze sacrificial place adjacent to the sanctuary. God's ownership and rule over the temple and its people are evident. God's instruction to measure the worshipers in the temple tells us that He protects His people, who are His church.

[16]"Do you not know that you are God's temple and that God's Spirit dwells in you? [17]If anyone destroys God's

temple, God will destroy him. For God's temple is holy, and you are that temple." (1 Corinthians 3:16-17).

[4]As you come to him, a living stone rejected by men but in the sight of God chosen and precious, 5you yourselves like living stones are being built up like a spiritual house, to be a holy priesthood, to offer spiritual sacrifices acceptable to God through Jesus Christ. [6]For it stands in Scripture: "Behold, I am laying in Zion a stone, a cornerstone chosen and precious, and whoever believes in him sill not be put to shame." So the honor is for you who believe, but for those who do not believe, The stone that the builders rejected has become the cornerstone." And A stone of stumbling, and a rock of offence. They stumble because they disobey the word, as they were destined to do." (1 Peter 2:4-8)

In Scripture, to take a measurement means that you are claiming possession. John is to measure, or count the believers, and God will claim possession. Scripture informs us that when the Great Tribulation begins, there will be a new temple in Jerusalem. John was not to measure the people or things in the court outside of this new temple. These people and things were "given over to the nations, and they will trample the holy city for forty-two months" (Revelation 11:2). The people referenced are the Gentiles and the unbelieving nations. The "forty-two months" are the first half of the Great Tribulation. There will be two witnesses who will prophesy while the Holy City of Jerusalem is trampled and destroyed. "And I will grant authority to my two witnesses, and they will prophesy for 1,260 days, clothed in sackcloth" (Revelation 11:3).

It is debated among biblical scholars whether the appearance and works of the two witnesses will occur in the first half, the second half, or throughout the seven-year Great Tribulation. Based on the timing of their appearance and activity in Revelation, the correct answer is the first half.

The second half of the Great Tribulation begins with the Antichrist ending the time of peace with Israel. He will usher in destruction and terror. The Antichrist will destroy the temple and declare himself to be God. However, God is faithful and orders the counting of His people, whom He still possesses.

> "And I lifted my eyes and saw, and behold, a man with a measuring line in his hand!
> Then I said, "Where are you going?" And he said to me, "To measure Jerusalem, to see what is its width and what is its length." And behold, the angel who talked with me came forward, and another angel came forward to meet him and said to him, "Run, say to that young man, Jerusalem shall be inhabited as villages without walls, because of the multitude of people and livestock in it. And I will be to her a wall of fire all around, declares the Lord, and I will be the glory in her midst." (Zechariah 1:12).

God will protect His church during times of trials. Furthermore, God will deliver His message of hope and salvation to the nonbelievers through the 144,000 Jewish evangelists. Additionally, Revelation 11:3 introduces God's two witnesses, who will be His special envoys. The witnesses will prophesy for twelve hundred and sixty days, or forty-two months. In a final expression of God's grace and mercy to repentant sinners, the two will proclaim the gospel, fulfilling a miraculous ministry similar to Moses and Elijah. The two witnesses are further identified in Revelation 11:4 as "the two olive trees and the two lampstands that stand before the Lord of the earth" (Revelation 11:4). Zechariah had a vision of the two olive trees and lampstands (Zechariah 4:1–14). Most biblical scholars believe these witnesses are two Jews of faith living at the time. God gave them great powers. They could "shut the skies of rain" and turn "water into blood," just as Moses turned the waters of the Nile into blood. As Elijah called down fire from heaven, they could call down fire to destroy their enemies and strike the earth with plagues. They had power over the water and performed many miracles, as recorded in Revelation 11:6.

The beast will soon rise up from the abyss to make war with the two witnesses and will kill them. God will leave their dead bodies in the streets for three and one-half days for the people to see. This will occur in Jerusalem, where the Lord was crucified. The city is called Sodom and Egypt because of its wickedness. The depraved will rejoice in the streets in Satanic celebrations. After three and one-half days, the Lord God will raise His two witnesses from their Death. In a loud voice for all to hear, God will call them up to heaven, and a great earthquake will strike the earth, killing seven thousand. The survivors will worship God in heaven.

The Seventh Trumpet

[15] Then the seventh angel blew his trumpet, and there were loud voices in heaven, saying, "The Kingdom of the world has become the kingdom of our Lord and of his Christ, and he shall reign forever and ever." [16]And the twenty-four elders who sit on their thrones before God fell on their faces and worshiped God,[17]saying,"We give thanks to you, Lord God Almighty, who is and who was, for you have taken your great power and begun to reign.[18]The nations raged, but your wrath came, and the time for the dead to be judged,
and for rewarding your servants and prophets and saints, and those who fear your name,
both small and great, and for destroying the destroyers of the earth." [9]Then God's temple in heaven was opened, and the ark of his covenant was seen within his temple.   There were flashes of lightning, rumblings, peals of thunder, an earthquake, and heavy hail.

God, the Almighty Father of us all, sees all that is past, present, and future. The seventh angel sounded his trumpet, and there was rejoicing in heaven. We read that the Lord God Almighty has begun to reign. Yet there are seven more bowl judgments to come from the Lord.

The twenty-four elders fell on their faces in worship because the Lord displayed His great power and began to reign. The twenty-four represent all of God's redeemed, including the Church and the redeemed of Israel. They rejoiced because the kingdom of the earth has become the kingdom of the Lord our God. Almighty God is eternal; He is the Lord of the past, present, and what is to come. The purity of the rejoicing in heaven is in contrast to the continued sin on earth. The

Great Tribulation is continuing on earth. Sinners rebel, and their rage only increases.

In Revelation 11:15, God gives His assurance to all believers. Whatever God calls us to do during our earthly journey, we are protected. Jesus said in Matthew 10:28, "Do not fear those who kill the body but cannot kill the soul." Jesus will return, and Death shall have no sting.

Thus, the sound of the seventh trumpet (Revelation 11:15) marks the beginning of the events leading to the triumphant return to the earth of Jesus. Christ will return to establish and rule His millennial kingdom. The judgments associated with the sound of the trumpet and the upcoming return of Christ are still in the future but vividly foretold in Revelation 11. It is in this reflective and informative pause in the pace of God's revelation to John that we take a respite for hope and thanksgiving. Judgments will resume shortly as the redemptive history of Christ continues to be revealed. Christ's kingdom has arrived, but more time must elapse before His kingdom is fully known and lived on earth. The millennial kingdom will come. It will become one with the eternal kingdom of our Lord God. The twenty-four elders, as members of the already raptured Church, will already be living this promise (Revelation 5:8).

John is shown God's temple in heaven, and in it, he sees the ark of the covenant. The ark represents God's union with the saved. It was on the ark where sacrifices were offered for the forgiveness of sin (Leviticus 16:2–16; Hebrews 9:3–7). God spoke to Moses from above the ark. In the Old Testament, the ark is also called the ark of testimony (Exodus 25:22) and the ark of God (1 Samuel 3:3). Throughout time, God has protected His Church. Despite flashes of lightning, thunder, earthquakes, hail, suffering, and earthly Death, there is heavenly life for the believer. Indescribable power, glory, awe, and joy await the faithful. Christians were being severely persecuted at the time of the writing of Revelation. Persecution of the believers will continue until the day of the new earth.

The great tragedy is that while the saints in heaven rejoice, the sinners of the earth fall further into defiance, rage, and sin. Sinners will have no desire to repent. Rather, their rage will worsen. Sinners of the earth will fall only deeper into the abyss.

> "[9]There will be tribulation and distress for every human being who does evil, the Jew first and also the Greek, [10]but glory and honor and peace for everyone who does good, the Jew first and also the Greek. [11]For God shows no partiality." (Romans 2:9-11).

When the seventh trumpet sounds, God will pour out His wrath on the unrepentant sinners. The time for redemption has passed for the unrepentant sinners, who will be judged along with the dead. God will reward the prophets, saints, believers, and all those who fear His name. Jesus told us repeatedly to watch and be ready, for the time is near.

Chapter 14

The Woman and the Dragon

The Woman and the Dragon

12 And a great sign appeared in heaven: a woman clothed with the sun, with the moon under her feet, and on her head a crown of twelve stars. [2]She was pregnant and was crying out in birth pains and the agony of giving birth. [3]And another sign appeared in heaven: behold, a great red dragon, with seven heads and ten horns, and on his heads seven diadems. [4]His tail swept down a third of the stars of heaven and cast them to the *earth. And the dragon stood before the woman who was about to give birth, so that when she bore her child he might devour it. [5]She gave birth to a male child, one who is to rule all the nations with a rod of iron, but her child was caught up to God and to his throne, [6]and the woman fled into the wilderness, where she has a place prepared by God, in which she is to be nourished for 1,260 days.

John's next vision was the appearance of a great sign in heaven. This is the first of seven signs in the second three and one-half years, the last half of Revelation. The vision is that of a mother who symbolizes Israel, "clothed with the sun, and the moon under her feet, and a crown of twelve stars" (Revelation 12:1). She was with child. The woman is not symbolic of the church, but rather of Israel. Her church is described in Scripture as the bride of Christ. Her labor pain results in the birth of a boy, who is our Lord Jesus Christ.

The next sign from heaven is a red dragon with seven heads, ten horns, and seven diadems on his heads. The dragon is Satan and was the vision of the Antichrist in Daniel 7. The ten horns of the dragon represent the ten nations over which the Antichrist will rule (Revelation 17:12). The dragon sought to kill the child, reminiscent of Genesis 3:15, but He was "caught up to God and to His throne." Thus, the Child is the Christ Child, our Lord and Savior.

John is shown the original fall of Satan as recorded in Isaiah 14 and Ezekiel 28. When the dragon wiped out one-third of the stars of heaven with his tail, God threw down to the earth Lucifer and the angels aligned with him (Daniel 8:10, 2 Peter 2:4, Jude 6). Lucifer became man's adversary. He became Satan. John saw all this.

Satan thrown Down to Earth

[7]Now war arose in heaven, Michael and his angels fought back,[8]but he was defeated, and there was no longer any place for them in heaven. [9]And the great dragon was thrown down, that ancient serpent, who is called the devil and Satan, the deceiver of the whole world-he was thrown down to the earth, and his angels were thrown down with him. [10]And I heard a loud voice in heaven, saying "Now the salvation and the power and the kingdom of our God and the authority of Christ have come, for the accuser of our brothers has been thrown down, who accuses them day and might before our God. [11]And they have conquered him by the blood of the lamb and by the word of their testimony, for they loved not their lives even unto Death.[12]Therefore, rejoice, O heavens and you who dwell in them! Bit woe to. You O earth and sea, for the devil has come down to you in great wrath, because he knows that his time is short!" [13]And when the dragon saw that he had been thrown down to the earth, he pursued the woman who had given birth to the male child. [14]But the woman was given the

two wings of the great eagle so that she might fly from the serpent into the wilderness, to the place where she is to be nourished for a time, and times, and half a time.[15]The serpent poured water like a river out of his mouth after the woman, to sweep her away with a flood.[16]But the earth came to the help of the woman, and the earth opened up its mouth and swallowed the river that the dragon had poured from his mouth.[17]Then the dragon became furious with the woman and went off to make war on the rest of her offspring, on those who keep the commandments of God and hold to the testimony of Jesus. And he stood on the sand of the sea.

The Archangel Michael and his angels waged war on the dragon in heaven. Michael's army triumphed over Satan and threw the dragon and his fallen angels down to the earth (Revelation 12:7–9). Michael, the commander of God's army, is the great prince. Satan is still in heaven for the time being. Hell has not yet been created by God. The spiritual war, which occupies all Christians who compose God's army, will continue until the end of days.

"And I heard a loud voice in heaven, saying "Now the salvation and the power and the kingdom of our God and the authority of Christ have come, for the accuser of our brothers has been thrown down, who accuses them day and might before our God. And they have conquered him by the blood of the lamb and by the word of their testimony." (Revelation 12:10-11).

Rejoicing continued in Heaven. The martyrs in haven sang a continual song of praise.

"Notice that the tribulation martyrs overcame Satan in three ways: First, they overcame because pf *"the blood of the Lamb."* They relied on the Death of Jesus, and that's why they are in heaven. Second, they overcame because of *"the word of their testimony."* They were active witnesses of the Lamb. Finally, they overcame because "they *did not love their life even when faced with Death."* They were willing to be martyrs rather than deny Christ. Jesus said in Matthew 10:39, "He who has found his life will lose it, and he who has lost his life for My sake will find it." (Jeffress p. 187).

Much more is recorded in Scripture of Satan's battles. He tried to destroy the birth of Christ. He tried to engineer the murder of David by Saul (1 Samuel 15:8–11). He led Herod in the murder of all males under two years of age in Bethlehem (Matthew 2:16), and more. Satan has never stopped. The Lord will triumph over Satan. Archangel Michael and his army of angels will defeat the dragon.

In verse 12:6, Scripture leaps forward in time to the second half of the Great Tribulation, the final 1,260 days when Satan wages war on Israel. These three and one-half years will be a time of unprecedented persecution of Israel. God promises that He will prepare shelter for the Israelites in the wilderness. God will protect His people with nourishment and safe haven, as we see in His protection of the woman in the wilderness. She was given two wings of the eagle, which is a metaphor from Exodus 19:4: "How I bore you on eagles' wings and brought you to myself." Some speculate that her shelter will be in Petra, the city of rocks. The woman was nourished, and her male child, who will rule all nations, was caught up to the heavens by God. However, the dragon was frustrated and will make war on the rest of the woman's offspring—that is, the church and Israel through the ages.

The dragon, or Satan, was defeated by Michael and his angels in heaven and "thrown down to earth" (Revelation 12:7–9). In Revelation 12:13–17, we see Satan's forces wage war on Israel during the Tribulation. Satan attacked the "woman who gave birth to the male child" (Revelation 12:13). The woman was given two wings of the great eagle and flew to safe shelter. Satan was thwarted in all his attempts to harm the woman. In a rage, Satan went off to make war against all her offspring and all those faithful to the commandments. He stood on the sands of the sea. Satan makes three attacks, and all were thwarted: defeated by Michael; the woman was saved from harm on eagles' wings; the serpent, Satan, poured out a river of water from his mouth to sweep her away; and he tried to make war against her children. Satan's efforts were all thwarted by the angels of heaven.

The final battle on earth commences with Satan unleashing his full fury on Israel, the chosen people of God. With the return of the Antichrist, many Jews fled into the wilderness. Some speculate this was to mountains in Petra. This is the time of the "abomination of desolation". In Revelation 12:14, this is the time when the woman, symbolic of Israel, will be carried to safety on the wings of a great eagle. God will lift up His people on eagles' wings, and the earth will swallow up the river from the serpent's mouth (Revelation 12:15). Throughout Scripture, wings symbolize strength, speed, and protection. The Jews will be saved from Satan's attacks. In the final three and one-half years of the Tribulation, God's chosen people will be saved.

> "For I am sure that neither Death nor life, nor angels nor rulers, nor things present nor things to come, nor powers, nor height nor depth, nor anything else in all creation, will be able to separate us from the love of God in Christ Jesus our Lord." (Romans 8:38-39).

Chapter 15

The First Beast

The First Beast

13 And I saw a beast rising out of the sea, with ten horns and seven heads, with ten diadems on its horns and blasphemous names on its heads. ² And the beast that I saw was like a leopard; its feet were like a bear's, and its mouth was like a lion's mouth. And to it the dragon gave his power and his throne and great authority. ³One of its heads seemed to have a mortal wound, but its mortal wound was healed, and the whole earth marveled as they followed the beast. ⁴And they worshiped the dragon, for he had given his authority to the beast, and they worshiped the beast saying, "Who is like the beast, and who can fight against it?" ⁵And the beast was given a mouth uttering haughty and blasphemous words, and it was allowed to exercise authority for forty-two months. ⁶It opened its mouth to utter blasphemies against God, blaspheming his name and his dwelling, that is, those who dwell in heaven. ⁷Also it was allowed to make war on the saints and to conquer them. And authority was given it over every tribe and people and language and nation, ⁸and all who dwell on earth will worship it, everyone whose name has not been written before the foundation of the world in the book of life of the Lamb who was slain. ⁹If anyone has an ear, let him hear" ¹⁰If anyone is to be taken captive, to captivity he goes; if anyone is to be slain with the sword, with the sword must he be slain.

The Second Beast

[11]Then I saw another beast rising out of the earth. It had two horns like a lamb. And it spoke like a dragon. [12]It exercises all the authority of the first beast in its presence, and makes the earth and its inhabitants worship the first beast, whose mortal wound was healed. [13]It performs great sighs, even making fire come down from heaven to earth in front of people,[14]and by the signs. That it is allowed to work in the presence if the beast it deceives those who dwell on earth, telling them to make an image for the beast that was wounded by the sword and yet lived.[15]And it was allowed to give breath to the image of the beast, so that the image of the beast might even speak and might cause those who would not worship the image of the beast to be slain.[16]Also it causes all, both small and great, both rich and poor, both free and slave, to be marked on the right hand or the forehead,[17]so that no one can buy or sell unless he has the mark, that is, the name of the beast or the number of his name. [18]This calls for wisdom: let the one who has the understanding calculate the number of the beast, for it is the number of a man and his number is 666.

John MacArthur describes the opening verses of Revelation 13 "as the most gripping, thorough, and dramatic in all of Scripture." (MacArthur, p. 213). Satan tries to outmaneuver God by establishing his kingdom on earth, led by the Antichrist, before Jesus Christ can establish God's new Kingdom on earth. The vivid descriptions of Satan's terrors are so powerful that many fear or doubt the Revelation to John. Revelation 12 ends with Satan being thrown down from the celestial heaven to earth. However, Satan's ferocity and his crowning as the Antichrist are no match for the power of our God.

The Tribulation will be so terrifying and painful that the people will willingly give up their freedom for the security that will be promised by a beast who will come out of the sea. The Great Tribulation will be the final seven years of the history of the planet Earth as we know it today.

The Antichrist was prophesied by Daniel.

> And he shall make a strong covenant with many for one week, and for half of one week he shall put an end to sacrifice and offering. And on the wing of abominations shall come one who makes desolate until the decreed end is poured out on the desolator." (Daniel 9:27)

In Revelation 13:1-4, we read that Satan, the dragon, stood on the sand of the sea, and as if on command, out of the sea rose a beast, the Antichrist. The sea is used as a metaphor in the Old Testament as a center for satanic activity (Job, Psalms, Isaiah). Satan stands in the midst of the sands of the sea as representative of the world's nations. "Most manuscripts read 'he stood,' referring again to the dragon, or Satan" (The MacArthur Study Bible, New King James Version, Thomas Nelson, Inc., Nashville, Tennessee, Second Edition, 2019, Revelation 10:13, p. 1839). A monstrous beast, with a powerful and terrifying appearance, rose from the ocean's depths. It is a killing machine.

The living saints are called upon to endure and remain faithful until the end. The beast, or Antichrist, rises out of the sea at a time when the world will be in turmoil. Those remaining on the earth will be fearful and angry. They have suffered from the outpouring of God's wrath and the ensuing chaos and Death. Initially, the people will be attracted to and readily accept the beast as their world leader. They will embrace him. He will have an extraordinary appearance and impact. He will be attractive and eloquent to a degree unlike any prior world leader.

Will all of humanity suffer this wrath of God delivered by the Antichrist? No. Christ's church is already raptured to the clouds of heaven and will not be punished.

> "At the rapture, millions of Christians will suddenly disappear. The world will be thrown into chaos, and out of that will emerge the Antichrist, who will promise peace. Revelation 6:2 pictures him as the rider on the white horse who has a bow but no arrows. He needs no force to take world power because he will be able to bring order out of disorder." ("Final Conquest", Pathway to Victory, Dallas, Texas, Copyright 2020, Dr. Robert Jeffress, P. 195).

We read that Satan will disguise himself as "an angel of light" in (2 Corinthians 11:4). The Antichrist will be irresistibly attractive to those living during the tribulation. It is clearly written that the Antichrist will have a global following. Those living during the tribulation will feel alone following the instantaneous pretribulation rapture of the church and will be frightened by the explosion of sin, Death, evil, mayhem, and crime. They will latch onto the charismatic Antichrist as a drowning sailor clings to his sinking ship. The Antichrist will be Satan's "last chance". Initially, he will be the most charismatic and convincing ambassador of Satan known by humankind. He will be Satan's greatest deceiver. There will be some Jews and Gentiles who will come to Christ during the seven years.

In Scripture, the nations of the Gentiles are represented by the sea. The Antichrist will rise out of the sea. The prophet Daniel had a vision of four beasts that "came up from the great sea" (Daniel 7:2–3). Daniel's beasts represented the Gentile nations of Babylon, Medo-Persia, Greece, and Rome. Thus, the Antichrist will be a Gentile.

The beast will have an extraordinary appearance. It will have ten horns, symbolic of his rule over the ten kings and their ten nations (Revelation 17:12). The horns are adorned with ten diadems, the jeweled crowns worn by sovereign leaders. Horns are a biblical sign of great strength. The number ten matches the visions of the fourth beast in Daniel.

The number ten is also symbolic of all the world's power and might. The beast will assume authority and rule over all. The beast will also have seven heads. The seven heads bear "blasphemous names" that represent total disrespect and rejection of God (Revelation 13:1). The beast will be like a leopard with the feet of a bear and the mouth of a lion. He will be like the fiercest animals in God's creation. In Daniel 7, the leopard represents Greece, the bear Medo-Persia, and the lion Babylon. The Antichrist will claim to be God himself. Daniel wrote that the Antichrist shall "exalt and magnify himself above every god, shall speak blasphemies against the God of gods, and shall prosper until the wrath has been accomplished." (Daniel 11:36).

The beast has a large visible wound on one of its heads. The wound is healed. We do not know if this severe head wound is an indication that the beast had been resurrected from the dead. If the healed wound is a mark from Satan, it could be that its purpose is to ensure that the people would readily follow the beast. Some believe that the beast's wound is a satanic imitation of Christ's wounds on the cross and His resurrection. John writes that all who live on the earth at the time will be deceived by the false prophet and the beast, with the only exceptions being the living believers. As the power of the Antichrist grows, there will be a satanic expansion of false religious worship of the Antichrist. He will escalate his blasphemous teaching, idolatry, and satanic deception. The Antichrist will take the lives of those who resist him.

The people worshiped the dragon in Revelation 13:4 for giving authority to the beast, and they worshiped the beast who appeared invincible because of his healed head wound. The people cried out in their worship of the Antichrist, saying, "Who is like the beast, and who is able to wage war with him?" (Revelation 13:4). The Antichrist was also given a mouth from which he uttered blasphemous words. He was allowed to exercise his authority and power at will. The Antichrist is operating under the brokered peace treaty first revealed in Daniel 9:27 for the first half, or forty-two months, of the Great Tribulation. The Antichrist is given authority over every nation and people, and to make war and crush the saints (Revelation 13:7).

During this time, the Antichrist will win the minds and hearts of the people with his deceptions. He will also begin his war, overcoming saints. The Antichrist will blaspheme the name of God and His tabernacle. In 2 Thessalonians 2:4, we read that the Antichrist "who opposes and exalts himself against every so-called god or object of worship, so that he takes his seat in the temple of God, proclaiming himself to be God."

The world will follow the Antichrist. The seven years of the tribulation will steadily increase in abomination so that those living through it will rush to and throw their allegiance to this charismatic and powerful leader. The people will surrender all their power to the Antichrist. "And they worshiped the dragon, for he had given his authority to the beast, and they worshiped the beast, saying, 'Who is like the beast, and who can fight against it?' (Revelation 13:4).

The Antichrist will spend his time on earth blaspheming God and attacking God's people. He will deceive the entire world, and all will worship him. To rule over all, the Antichrist will make war with the saints (Revelation 13:7). He will sit in the temple of God and present himself to the multitudes as God. At the midpoint in the seven-year Great Tribulation, he will break his peace treaty with Israel, name himself and present himself as God, and fully engage in warfare against the saints. After first rebuilding the temple in Jerusalem, the Antichrist will destroy it in the second forty-two months of the Great Tribulation. In Revelation

13:8, we read that all who dwell on the earth will worship the beast, and every person whose name is not written in the book of life will be slain.

Believers are safe. By God's grace, our names have been written in the book of life since the beginning of time. Christ promised His believers eternal life. The doctrine of the perseverance of the saints promises that believers will persevere in faith until the end.

The Antichrist will blaspheme God, God's name, and His tabernacle. He will claim to be God himself. He will attack the church and believers, even to the point of murder. Both Jewish and Gentile believers will be the Antichrist's victims. Despite this horror, and because of the evil power of the Antichrist, the nonbelievers will still worship him. Again, nothing the Antichrist can do to believers will keep them from salvation. The saints will always be saved by their faith.

As the end approaches, the Antichrist will turn his wickedness on the living believers. Jews and Gentiles who will be saved during the Great Tribulation will die at the hands of the Antichrist. "Here is a call for the endurance and faith of the saints." (Revelation 13:10).

Three demons—Satan, the Antichrist, and the false prophet—comprise a satanic trinity. The false prophet will assist the Antichrist in his ascent to power. The false prophet is the second beast. This second beast is not as frightening as the first beast. He has but two horns as his symbols of power. He presides over a religious and political empire.

As the third member of the satanic trinity, the second beast is empowered by Satan. He will assist the Antichrist in his evil works. He came up out of the earth, not out of the sea, and thus will not be as frightful or feared as the Antichrist. Having but two horns, he will have just two sources of power. He will rule over a political and religious empire, conducting his affairs with gentleness and peacefulness. His words attract followers. When the people come to follow him, they will be following the Antichrist as well.

He presides over an apostate church that will be destroyed by the Antichrist when he destroys the temple he had rebuilt in Jerusalem. He demands that the people worship the Antichrist. He calls fire down from heaven. He is a great deceiver and serves as the Antichrist's spokesman. He ordered that an image of the Antichrist be made and placed in the temple of Jerusalem. The image will appear lifelike, even speaking and giving orders to kill those who do not worship the Antichrist.

The false prophet will brand all worshipers of the Antichrist with the mark 666 on their forehead or right hand to identify them as worshipers of the Antichrist. Those without such a mark will be in jeopardy. They will be unable to make any financial transactions, such as buying food. Believers who refuse the mark will suffer, but their suffering will be wiped away by their eternal salvation.

Chapter 16

The Lamb and the 144,000

The Lamb and the 144,000

14 Then I looked, and behold, on Mount Zion stood the Lamb, and with him 144,000 who had his name and his Father's name written on their foreheads. [2]And I heard a voice from heaven like the roar of many waters and like the sound of loud thunder. The voice I heard was like the sound of harpists playing on their harps, [3]and they were singing a new song before the throne and before the four living creatures and before the elders. No one could learn that song except the 144,000 who had been redeemed from the earth. [4]It is these who have not defiled themselves with women, for they are virgins. It is these who follow the Lamb wherever he goes. These have been redeemed from mankind as firstfruits for God and the Lamb, [5]and in their mouth no lie was found, for they are blameless.

The Messages of the Three Angels

[6]Then I saw another angel flying directly overhead, with an eternal gospel to proclaim to those who dwell on earth, to every nation and tribe and language and people. [7]And he said with a loud voice, "Fear God and give him glory, because the hour of his judgement has come, and worship him who made heaven and earth, the sea and the springs of water." [8]Another angel, a second followed, saying, "Fallen, fallen is Babylon the great, she who made all nations drink the wine of passion of her sexual immorality." [9]And another angel, a third, followed the saying with a loud voice, "If anyone

worships the beast and its image and receives a mark on his forehead or on his hand, [10]he also will drink the wine of God's wrath, poured full strength into the cup of his anger, and he will be tormented with fire and sulfur in the presence of the holy angels and in the presence if the Lamb. [11]And the smoke of their torment goes up forever and ever, and they have no rest, day or night, these worshipers of the beast and its image, and whoever receives the mark of its name." [12]Here is a call for the endurance of the saints, those who keep the commandments of God and their faith in Jesus. [13]And I heard a voice from heaven saying, "Write this: Blessed are the dead who die in the Lord from now on." "Blessed indeed," says the Spirit, "that they may rest from their labors, for their deeds follow them!"

The Harvest of the Earth

[14]Then I looked, and behold, a white cloud, and seated on the cloud one like a son of man, with a golden crown on his head, and a sharp sickle in his hand. [15]And another angel came out of the temple, calling with a loud voice to him who sat on the cloud, "Put in your sickle, and reap, for the hour to reap has come, for the harvest of the earth is fully ripe." [16]So he who sat on the cloud swung his sickle across the earth, and the earth was reaped. [17]Then another angel came out of the temple in heaven, and he too had a sharp sickle. [18]And another angel came out from the altar, the angel who has authority over the fire, and he called with a loud voice to the one who had the sharp sickle, "Put in your sickle and gather the clusters from the vine of the earth, for its grapes are ripe." [19]So the angel swung his sickle across the earth and gathered the grape harvest of the earth and threw it into the great winepress of the wrath of God. [20]And the winepress was trodden outside the city, and

blood flowed from the winepress, as high as a horse's bridle, for 1,600 stadia.

The next thing that John tells us about his vision is that he looked and saw the Lamb standing on Mount Zion with an army of 144,000 Jewish evangelists and believers in Christ the Messiah. Mount Zion was the ancient name of Jerusalem. The capital city of ancient Jerusalem will also be the capital city of the new millennial kingdom to come. The Lamb is Jesus. The 144,000 survived the actions of Satan and the judgments of God on the world and its sinners during the Great Tribulation. They will be marked with God's seal on their foreheads. The Lamb's name and His Father's name will be written on the foreheads of the 144,000, indicating they were the possession of and were protected by the Lord. Thus, the 144,000 will be protected during the Great Tribulation from torment and Death. No one will be able to harm them.

The 144,000 will not be the only ones saved during the tribulation. Many, perhaps multitudes, of Jews (Zechariah 12:10; 13:1, 9; Romans 11:26–27) and Gentiles (Revelation 6:9–11; 7:9, 13–17; Matthew 25:31–46) will be saved. However, thousands upon thousands will die as martyrs from the unimaginable terrors of the Antichrist during the Great Tribulation. When Jesus returns to earth in His second coming, or the Parousia, He will stand upon Mount Zion with the 144,000 standing by His side.

John has a vision of three angels who are coming to announce imminent judgment. "Blessed are the dead who die in the Lord from now on. 'Blessed indeed,' says the Spirit, 'that they may rest from their labors, for their deeds follow them!'" (Revelation 14:13). Three angels will announce, and three other angels will execute, the harvest of man on earth. In the midst of these angels, John sees the Son of Man who gathers grain from the earth. We are told that the martyrs are blessed in their Death, for they died in the Lord and are resting from their labors.

John hears the 144,000 "singing a new song before the throne and before the four living creatures". The new song likely praises God's victory over sin through the Lamb and His sacrifice. The chorus of 144,000 are also likely singing thanksgiving for their redemption. No one else present could learn this song. It was a song of praise for the redemptive work of Jesus Christ. They were obedient to Jesus, sexually pure, purchased by God, and the "first fruits of the Lamb" (Revelation 14:4). Redeemed by Christ's blood, the 144,000 are to serve a special ministry during the Great Tribulation. The worship of the Antichrist and his vile deeds will be indescribable terrors during this time. The 144,000 and the Tribulational martyrs will be beacons of light and faith for all living believers. They are to speak, spread, and praise the truths given to them by God. They will utter no untruths. They will save souls by their faithfulness to Christ as they "follow the Lamb wherever He goes" (Revelation 14:4). They will be like the first fruits offered in Deuteronomy 18:3–5.

God continues to bless His people and warn them of the deception, enemies, and dangers to come. God is forever faithful to us.

The 144,000 remain "blameless" and pure. They stand blameless before God. As such, they are the "first fruits for God and the Lamb" (Revelation 14:4), the first believers to be harvested by the Lord. They are undefiled virgins who will follow the Lamb wherever He goes.

During the tribulation, God will send three angels with messages that the Lord God is to be feared and worshiped. His judgment is to come. All people on earth should praise God, for He created everything. All people should also fear God, for He will crush the wicked and punish sin. Those living have time to repent and be forgiven. The first angel proclaims the eternal gospel, bringing its message of hope. Each of us is called to repent and praise the Lord our God in song, word, thought, and action. We are to preach the Gospel to "every nation and tribe". (Revelation 14:6–7). This is the same message of Matthew 24:14, where Jesus said, "And this gospel of the kingdom will be proclaimed throughout the whole world as a testimony to all nations, and then the end will come."

An angel flies overhead and commands in a loud voice, "Fear God and give Him glory, because the hour of His judgment has come, and worship Him who made heaven and earth, the sea and the springs of water." (Revelation 14:6–7). The angel suggests that the reign of God and Christ on earth is arriving soon. Three angels will announce God's judgment and the fall of Babylon, with eternal punishment for the Beast and its followers.

A second angel announces the coming destruction with the warning that Babylon fell because of its paganism, such as sexual immorality. Ancient Babylon captured Judah. King David, and thus Jesus, were of the Tribe of Judah. Rome was another great pagan power with "dominion over the kings of earth" and persecuted Christ's people. This alarm does not appear to be limited to the ancient kingdom of Babylon but rather cries out as an admonition against the world's opposition to God and its addiction to sin. The sinful passions of man for prosperity, immorality, and pleasures of the flesh are adultery against God. Time has arrived for God's reckoning.

The second angel delivers the message that the world opposed to God will be destroyed. Death and eternal suffering will come to those who refuse to repent of their sin. The second angel is sent by God to warn the people. This is a last call from God. Clearly, the multitudes have not heeded God's warnings or history. We know this to be the world's history. Tragically for the sinners, nothing has changed.

The third angel is sent to deliver a terrifying message of doom to the unrepentant, the wicked, and especially to anyone who worships the Antichrist and takes the mark of the beast. We know that those who refuse the beast's mark will suffer wrath and Death at the hand of the Antichrist. However, this temporary suffering will be completely washed away by eternal salvation. Those who take the beast's mark will be damned to the eternal fires of hell. Worshiping the Antichrist will be like drinking the eternal wrath of God. "The wine of God's wrath, poured full strength into the cup of His anger, and he will be tormented with fire and sulfur in the presence of the holy angels and in the presence of the Lamb. And the smoke of their torment goes up forever and ever, and they have no rest, day or night, these worshipers of the beast and its image, and whoever receives the mark of its name." (Revelation 14:10–11) with its "fire and sulfur" night and day, forever and ever. (Revelation 14: 9-11). The rising smoke of their torment will continue for eternity. Hell is eternal.

These three angels deliver the final warning. It will be the last chance at redemption for unrepentant sinners. God does not tire or become discouraged. He is giving creation thousands of years to repent, beginning with original sin in the garden. When His patience ends, He will eternally crush Satan and unrepentant sinners. There will be glory and righteousness in the new heaven and the new earth to come.

The angels' final warning is now delivered, and John is told what will come next in a fourth announcement. He hears a voice from heaven instructing him to write, "Blessed are the dead who die in the Lord from now on. 'Blessed indeed,' says the Spirit, 'that they may rest from their labors, for their deeds follow them!'" (Revelation 14:13). What we do on earth is recorded in heaven. Our deeds will not be forgotten, nor will good deeds go unrewarded. Those who repent of their sin will know eternal paradise. Martyrs will know God's blessings for eternity. All the faithful living at the time of the Great Tribulation and every martyr will know eternal blessing in the Lord.

We read in Scripture and often hear in daily discourse, "Blessed is he who keeps the commandments of the Lord." Scripture tells us to be faithful and to endure. Those who do will be spared the horrors that come next as God pours out His wrath.

It is time to harvest in Revelation 14:14–20. Jesus the Christ takes up His sickle. This time, the Son of Man, with a crown of gold and seated on a cloud holding a sickle as if a farmer, is prepared to harvest wheat. An angel calls out to Christ, "Put in your sickle and reap, for the hour to reap has come, for the harvest of the earth is fully ripe." (Revelation 14:15). Jesus swung His sickle, and "the earth was reaped".

Jesus, the Son of Man, might gather believers and saints, lifting them to salvation. Another possible outcome is that Jesus will call sinners to judgment.

The harvest being of wheat seems consistent with saving believers from further tribulation. The prophet Joel offers the alternate understanding. Prophets deliver God's Word. The prophetic book of Joel is focused on the Day of the Lord. Joel was also from Judah or possibly Jerusalem. Joel's prophecy fits well with Revelation 14.

> "Let the nations stir themselves up and come up to the Valley of Jehoshaphat; for there I will sit to judge all the surrounding nations. Put in the sickle, for the harvest is ripe. Go in, tread, for the winepress is full. The vats

overflow, for their evil is great. Multitudes, multitudes, in the valley of decision! For the day of the Lord is near in the valley of decision. The sun and the moon are darkened, and the stars withdraw their shining." (Joel: 3:12-15).

Next, an angel appears coming out of the temple in heaven with a sharp sickle in hand. Another angel comes out from the altar. The angel from the altar has power over fire. He calls out in a loud voice, "Put in your sickle and gather the clusters from the vine of the earth, for its grapes are ripe." (Revelation 14:18–19). The sickle was swung, and the harvest of the grapes of the earth was thrown into the "great winepress of the wrath of God". (Revelation 14:19). Blood flowed from the winepress as high as the bridle of a horse and covered a distance of 200 miles.

This is the vision of Daniel, who prophesied a similar second coming and the triumph of the Messiah.

"I saw in the night visions, and behold, with clouds of heaven there came one like a son of man, and he came to the Ancient of Days and was presented before him. And to him was given dominion and glory and a kingdom, that all peoples, nations, and languages should serve him; his dominion is an everlasting dominion, which shall not pass away, and his kingdom one that shall not be destroyed." (Daniel 7:13-14).

The Ancient of Days is the name of God. The Son of Man is Jesus. Centuries ago, the prophets were told of what is to come. God was using His prophets on earth to call man to salvation. Man must believe and repent in order to be saved.

The believers who are harvested off the earth will know eternity with the Lord. The unbelievers will be "harvested" off the earth and judged.

The harvest of the vines and the crushing of the grapes in the great winepress of the wrath of God, with the blood overflowing for two hundred miles, foretells the bloodbath that will take place in the Battle of Armageddon. This battle, which will be more fully prophesied in Revelation 19, will see the final destruction of the Antichrist and his armies by the hand of Jesus, our Lord and Savior, at His second coming.

It is tragic how sinners will cling to their sin. They will not repent. Thus, they will choose hell—eternal, indescribable suffering—over eternal salvation and joy. Even if believers were to only avoid the suffering and damnation of the sinners and not know eternal life in heaven, who would choose the life of sin? This repeated tragedy is the great deception of Satan. Praise the Lord that the saved will be blessed beyond human understanding for eternity.

Chapter 17

The Seven Angels with Seven Plagues

The Seven Angels with Seven Plagues

15 Then I saw another sign in heaven, great and amazing, seven angels with seven plagues, which are the last, for with them the wrath of God is finished. [2]And I saw what appeared to be a sea of glass mingled with fire - and also those who had conquered the beast and its image and the number of its name, standing beside the sea of glass with harps of God in their hands. [3]And they sing the song of Moses, the servant of God, and the song of the Lamb, saying, "Great and amazing are your deeds, O Lord God the Almighty! Just and true are your ways, O King of the nations! Who will not fear, O Lord, and glorify your name? For you alone are holy. All nations will come and worship you, or your righteous acts have been revealed." [5]After this I looked, and the sanctuary of the tent of witness in heaven opened, [6]and out of the sanctuary came the seven angels with the seven plagues, clothed in pure, bright linen, with golden sashes around their chests. [7]And one of the four living creatures gave to the seven angels seven golden bowls full of the wrath of God who lives forever and ever, [8]and the sanctuary was filled with smoke from the glory of God and from his power, and no one could enter the sanctuary until the seven plagues of the seven angels were finished.

Chapter 18

The Seven Bowls of God's Wrath

The Seven Bowls of God's Wrath

16 Then I heard a loud voice from the temple telling the seven angels, "Go and pour out on the earth the seven bowls of the wrath of God." [2]So the first Angel went and poured out his bowl on the earth, and harmful and painful sores came upon the people who bore the mark of the beast and worshiped its image. [3]The second angel poured out his bowl into the sea, and it became like the blood of a corpse, and every living thing died that was in the sea. [4]The third angel poured out his bowl into the rivers and the springs of water and they became blood. [5]And I heard the angel in charge of the waters say, "Just are you, O Holy One, who is and who was, for you brought these judgements. For they have shed the blood of saints and prophets, and you have given them blood to drink. It is what they deserve!" And I heard the altar saying, "Yes, Lord God the Almighty, true and just are your judgments!" [8]The fourth angel poured out his bowl on the sun, and it was allowed to scorch people with fire. [9]They were scorched by the fierce heat, and they cursed the name of God who had power over these plagues. They did not repent and give him glory. [10]The fifth angel poured out his bowl on the throne of the beast, and its kingdom was plunged into darkness. People gnawed their tongues in anguish [11]and cursed the God of heaven for their pain and sores. They did not repent of their deeds.

[12]The sixth angel poured out his bowl on the great river Euphrates, and its water was dried up, to prepare the way for the kings from the east. [13]And I saw, coming out of the mouth of the dragon and out of the mouth of the beast and out of the mouth of the false prophet, three unclean spirits like frogs. [14]For they are demonic spirits, performing signs, who go abroad to the kings of the whole world, to assemble them for battle on the great day of God the Almighty. Behold, I am coming like a thief! Blessed is the one who stays awake keeping his garments on, that he may not go about naked and be seen exposed!"). [16]And they assembled them at the place that in Hebrew is called Armageddon.

The Seventh Bowl

The seventh angel poured out his bowl into the air, and a loud voice came out of the temple from the throne, saying, "It is done!" [18]And there were flashes of lightning, rumblings, peals of thunder, and a great earthquake such as there had never been since man was on the earth, so great was that earthquake. [19]Tbe great city was split into three parts, and the cities of the nations fell, and God remembered Babylon the great, to make her drain the cup of the wine of the fury of his wrath. [20]And every island fled away, and no mountains were to be found. [21] And great hailstones, about one hundred pounds each, fell from heaven on people; and they cursed God for the plague of the hail, because the plague was so severe.

God's outpouring of wrath on unrepentant sinners is on full display in Revelation 15 and 16. Known as the seven bowl Judgments, God will mete out severe punishment on unrepentant sinners who, along with the Antichrist, will be cast into hell for eternity. The seven bowl judgments, or "last plagues", that will be "thrown down" on the earth will be unlike anything ever known by man. These worldwide bowl judgments will begin at the end of the Great Tribulation, just before the Parousia—Christ's return to earth—and the Battle of Armageddon. We are spiraling closer every day to their arrival.

God is patient. There will be many who come to Christ and are saved during the Great Tribulation. However, many more will be unrepentant. God's patience will ultimately run out on the unrepentant, and thus they will be condemned to eternal suffering. God's last punishment on His creation will be His most fierce. "For with them, the wrath of God is finished." (Revelation 15:1). God will crush evil.

A prolonged wave of seven plagues is coming in punishment. The biblical term "plague" means either a supernatural disaster or the delivered judgment of God. Such a delivered judgment can mean a physical blow or a wound. Biblical plagues strike suddenly and decisively. The last plagues to come are known as the seven bowl judgments. They mark the completion of the delivery of God's wrath on sinners and the final triumph of Jesus Christ on earth. Many Christians struggle with the intensity of the wrath of God depicted in the Book of Revelation. God is a God of love and fidelity. He gave His only Son that we might live. However,

God punishes sin. We have seen this beginning in Genesis and continuing throughout the Bible. "The Lord is slow to anger and great in power, and the Lord will by no means clear the guilty." (Nahum 1:3).

In Revelation 15:2, John sees a sea of glass before the throne, before which the saints of the tribulation are standing. They are the ones who did not take the mark of the beast. They now stand victorious in heaven, singing praises to the Lord God. The sea of glass is transparent flooring or pavement surrounding the throne of God.

"And they saw the God of Israel. There was under his feet as it were a pavement of sapphire stone like the very heaven for clearness." (Exodus: 24:10).

Over the heads of the living creatures there was the likeness of an expanse, shining like awe-inspiring crustal, spread out above their heads." (Ezekiel 1:22)

Next, they sing the song of Moses, composed by Moses following the Israelites' safe passage through the Red Sea. This song praises God's power and His willingness to deliver His believers. The tribulation saints next sing the song of the Lamb, which is the last song that is sung in Scripture. It praises God for the triumph over Babylon. For now, Heaven's sanctuary is celebratory with songs of worship and praise for the Lamb's victory.

Revelation 15:5 tells us that "the sanctuary of the tent of witnesses in heaven was opened" (The Holy Bible, English Standard Version, Crossway, Wheaton, Illinois, 2001, p. 2484). The King James Version translation reads: "the temple of the tabernacle of the testimony in heaven was opened" (Holy Bible, King James Version, Christian Art Publishers, 2017, Vereeniging, p. 1730). The terms are synonymous. The "tent of witnesses" and "the temple of the tabernacle" are alternate terms for the Ark of the Covenant, the Law of God. It was the "holy of holies", and as such, was always kept in the most sacred part of the temple, as recorded in Old Testament writings. The seven angels coming out of the sanctuary of the tent that was opened indicated that their judgments were about to be meted out on the earth and creation. A "living creature" gave each of the seven angels a golden bowl containing the wrath of God in the form of a plague. "No one could enter the sanctuary until all seven plagues of the seven angels were finished." (Revelation 15:8). The seven angels were God's representatives and were clothed in bright linens adorned with golden sashes, indicating their regal stature. Each bowl contained a specific plague, or judgment, and was the punishment from God.

It is not too late for sinners. We are all sinners. If we stop immediately and confess to God with all our heart and all our mind that we are sinners and ask for the saving forgiveness of Christ, we will be saved immediately and forever.

The seven bowl judgments come rapidly and sequentially. The previous trumpet judgments each impacted one-third of the earth. The bowl judgments will follow each other quickly, and each will impact the entire world. However, the punishment of each bowl will target only those who wear the mark of the beast. Living believers saved in Christ will not suffer the bowl judgments. The severe seven bowl judgments will conclude God's judgments and end the world's history. The first heaven and earth will be destroyed. They will be replaced with something of unimaginable beauty and peace.

The first angel poured out his bowl on the earth, and those who wore the mark of the beast suffered painful, oozing boils and sores. The second angel poured his bowl into the sea, and it turned blood red. Every living thing in the sea was killed. The third angel emptied his bowl into the rivers and springs, and they, too, became blood. Those who shed the blood of the saints are then given blood to drink.

> "I will make your oppressors eat their own flesh, and they shall be drunk with their own blood as with wine. Then all flesh shall know that I am the Lord your Savior, and your Redeemer, the Mighty One of Jacob." (Isaiah 49:26).

The fourth angel poured his bowl on the sun, and it burned the people with fierce heat. The fifth angel poured his bowl on the throne of the beast, and the beast's kingdom was in darkness. The sixth angel poured his bowl into the Euphrates River, and its water dried up. The Euphrates was once a great river. Ancient Babylon relied on it for its defense against invasions. It later was the eastern boundary of the Roman Empire and kept the unfriendly Parthians at bay. The Lord creates rivers and just as easily can cause them to dry up. The dry Euphrates River bed will be repurposed by the Lord. It will be the Lord's pathway to the battle at Armageddon.

Then three unclean spirits like frogs assembled the kings and assembled the armies for battle at Armageddon.

The frogs are demonic spirits—filthy, sinful, and repulsive. They will be Satan's workers and assistants. Satan and the kings of the earth will join together to battle the Lord our God at Armageddon, hoping to destroy Israel and all Jews. The three frogs are suggestive of the "unholy trinity" of Satan, the Antichrist, and the false prophet. Evil will not prevail. God will assemble all the world's armies for one great and final battle.

This is the climax of the tribulation. In an instant, there will be no water, no sea life, scorching heat; darkness will fall on the beast and those who worship him! Battle lines will form. The martyrs in heaven will cry out in song and voice, praising God, who is great and just.

The seventh bowl will be the last expression of God's wrath on sinners. It will also be without equal when compared to God's previous outpourings of wrath. It will start with a cleansing of the air, perhaps to wash away the stench of evil and sin. It will be global. It will be so fierce that there will be a sense of doom. One-hundred-pound hailstones will fall down on men. Hailstones are recorded in Scripture as instruments of God's judgment. However, never before have hailstones been of giant proportion. Similarly, there will be an earthquake so powerful it will split Jerusalem into three parts. No earthquake has been or ever will be as powerful. Jerusalem was the location of Christ's crucifixion and also that of the martyrs. Its seismic division could be in preparation for Jerusalem's future role in the millennial kingdom. The Lord makes way for the new heaven and the new earth.

In a statement of finality, God will proclaim in a loud voice, "It is done". God's plan is complete. Isaiah 40:4 foretells that "Every valley shall be lifted up and every mountain and hill be made low." God's Word and God's plans always unfold as He tells us they will. Despite such terrors, once again, survivors will be unrepentant and blasphemous. In His grace, God is patient. We do not know His timing or the timing of Christ's return. We are repeatedly told in the gospels to be alert and to be ready.

Chapter 19

The Great Prostitution and the Beast

The Great Prostitute and the Beast

17 Then one of the seven angels who had the seven bowls came and said to me, "Come, I will show you the judgment of the great prostitute who is seated on many waters, ²with whom the kings of the earth have committed sexual immorality, and with the wine of whose sexual immorality the dwellers on earth have become drunk." ³And he carried me away in the spirit into a wilderness, and I saw a woman sitting on a scarlet beast that was full of blasphemous names, and it had seven heads and ten horns. ⁴The woman was arrayed in purple and scarlet, and adorned with gold and jewels and pearls, holding in her hand a golden cup full of abominations and impurities of her sexual immorality. ⁵And on her forehead as written a name of mystery: "Babylon the great, mother of prostitutes and of earth's abominations." ⁶And I saw the woman, drunk with the blood of the saints, the blood of the martyrs of Jesus. When I saw her, I marveled greatly. ⁷But the angel said to me, "Why do you marvel? I will tell you the mystery of the woman, and of the beast with seven heads and ten horns that carries her. ⁸The beast that you saw was, and is not, and is about to rise from the bottomless pit and go to destruction. And the dwellers on earth whose names have not been written in the book of life from the foundation of the world will marvel to see the beast, because it was and is not and is to come. ⁹This calls for a mind with wisdom: the seven heads are seven mountains on which the woman is seated; ¹⁰they are also seven kings, five of whom have fallen, one is, the other has not yet come, and when he does come he must remain only a little while. [11]As for the beast that was and is not, it is an eighth but belongs to the seven, and it goes to destruction. [12]And the ten horns that you saw are ten kings who have not yet received royal power, but they are to receive authority as kings for one hour, together with the beast. [13]These are of one mind, and they hand over their power and authority to the beast. [14]They will make war on the Lamb, and the Lamb will conquer them for he is Lord of lords and King of kings, and those with him are called and chosen and faithful." [15]And the angel said to me, "The waters that you saw, where the prostitute is seated, are peoples and multitudes and nations and languages. [16]And the ten horns that you saw, they and the beast will hate the prostitute. They will make her desolate and naked, and devour her flesh and burn her up with fire, [17]for God has put it into their hearts to carry out his purpose by being of one mind and handing over their royal power to the beast, until the words of God are fulfilled. [18]And the woman that you saw is the great city that has dominion over the kings of the earth."

Wilbur Smith, in the chapter "Revelation" in the Wycliffe Bible Commentary, noted that Babylon and the judgments of God that will be suffered are cited over forty times in Revelation. (Smith, Wilbur M., "Revelation", The Wycliffe Bible Commentary, pp. 1491–1525. Edited by Charles F. Pfeiffer and Everett F. Harrison. Chicago: Moody Press, 1962.). "Babylon," as used in Scripture, can refer to the city of Babylon, which was the ancient capital city of the Babylonian Empire, the city of Rome, (1 Peter 5:13), or a global system of governance and control. Dr. Robert Jeffress presents a strong argument that throughout Revelation,

"Babylon" refers to a worldwide system that will be ruled by the Antichrist. "Babylon" will become the empire of the Antichrist. It will develop into a global system encompassing the Antichrist's false religion, temporary global reign, fearsome power, and financial systems. (Final Conquest, Dr. Robert Jeffress, Pathway to Victory, 2020, pp. 246–271)

In Revelation 17:1, "one of the angels who had the seven bowls came to" John and offered to show John "the judgment of the great prostitute". The "great prostitute" has a broad meaning. It includes the false gods of Israel. It is a reference to "adulterous" practices toward God in false religions and all forms of immorality. Many religions in today's world separate people from God and salvation. Examples include aberrant Christian churches that preach the "name it and claim it" or "prosperity" gospels, Islam, Hinduism, and Mormonism. False religions will be with us until the final day of judgment on earth. Saint Paul wrote of this in his Second Letter to the Thessalonians.

> "[1]Now concerning the coming of our Lord Jesus Christ and our being gathered together to him, we ask you, brothers,[2]not to be quickly shaken in mind or alarmed either by the spirit or spoken word, or a letter seeming to be from us, to the effect that the day of the Lord has come. [3]Let no one deceive you in any way. For that day will not come, unless rebellion comes first, and the man of lawlessness is revealed, the son of destruction, [4]who opposes and exalts himself against every so-called god or object of worship, so that he takes his seat in the temple of God, proclaiming himself to be God. [5]Do you not remember that when I was still with you I told you

these things? [6]And you know what is restraining him now so that many be revealed in his time. [7]For the mystery of lawlessness is already at work. Only he who now restrains it will do so until he is out of the way. [8]And then the lawless one will be revealed, whom the Lord Jesus Christ will kill with the breath of his mouth and bring to nothing by the appearance of his coming. [9]The coming of the lawless one is by the activity of Satan with all power and false signs and wonders, and [10]with all wicked deception for those who are perishing, because they refused to love the truth and so be saved. [11]Therefore God sends them a strong delusion so that they may be believe what is false, [12]in order that all may be condemned who did not believe the truth but had pleasure in unrighteousness. (2 Thessalonians 2:1-12).

Paul wrote his second letter to the Thessalonian church from the city of Corinth in approximately the year A.D. 50. This young church was being influenced by false teachings of the day. Paul was fighting false religions and their attacks on the teachings of Christ and His one true religion. Paul is addressing one of the most dangerous of these false teachings, that the "day of the Lord", when Christ will return to earth for His final judgment of humankind, had already occurred. In this letter, Paul writes the truths we read again in The Revelation to John, written some forty-five years later, circa A.D. 96.

Paul's letter is prophetic. He is writing of things to come, as told directly to him by our Lord Jesus Christ during His time on earth. Paul writes of the Great Tribulation, the Antichrist (the man of lawlessness), and the rebellion to come. The rebellion will be against God and everything sacred. Man will descend further and further into sin. The Antichrist will emerge and be embraced by the masses as the saving leader. The Restrainer is the Holy Spirit, who has been present on earth since the Death of Christ. The Restrainer has been keeping Satan, the son of destruction, subdued. The Restrainer will continue His restraint of Satan until the rapture of the church is completed. At that time, the Antichrist will emerge, and the Great Tribulation begins. (Please see the author's previous publication The Gift of Salvation: Will You Be Raised Up to the Clouds of Heaven?)

Revelation 17 continues with the vision of the fall of Babylon, flowing from God's wrath seen in the angel's swing of the sickle and the winepress in verses 14:18–19. It is triggered by the seventh bowl and its lightning, thunder, and great earthquake in verses 16:18–19. "Babylon the Great" is the empire of the beast. It is presented in verses 18:1–8 as the great prostitute, who will ultimately fall.

John is told, "Come, I will show you the judgment of the great prostitute". This "great prostitute" refers to the spiritual sin and immorality of the belief system of Babylon—a false religious system over which the Antichrist will rule. Sexual immorality and spiritual infidelity are similar and perhaps intertwined. Babylon's sensuality and physical beauty are intoxicating, quite similar to contemporary society. The mind, heart, and body are often consumed by it (see Ezekiel 16:15–43).

Verse 17:3 tells us that John is transported by the Holy Spirit into the wilderness where he "saw a woman sitting on a scarlet beast". "Then the Spirit lifted me up, and I heard behind me the voice of a great earthquake: 'Blessed be the glory of the Lord from its place!' ... 'And the Spirit lifted me up and brought me in the vision by the Spirit of God into Chaldea to the exiles. Then the vision that I had seen went up from me." (Ezekiel 3:12, 11:24). Chaldea was located in ancient Mesopotamia. Written on the woman's forehead was the name "Babylon the Great, Mother of Prostitutes and of the Earth's Abominations." The woman "was drunk with the blood of the saints, the blood of the martyrs of Jesus." She was adorned in gold, jewels, and pearls, and dressed in purple and scarlet. She was an image of the seductive wealth and earthly values of both ancient and contemporary society. Being drunk with the blood of the saints, the martyrs of Jesus, tells us that, as with contemporary society, the society in John's vision is addicted to the pleasures of the flesh. Thus, it will cooperate with the government powers to quench the testimony to Christ by putting to Death His witnesses.

John's angelic guide, while showing the woman to him, cautioned John not to "marvel" at the woman. The angel told John that he would explain who she was and her mystery.

The great prostitute seated on many waters is explained to John by the angel in verse 17:15. It represents the multitude of peoples, nations, and languages. It is similar in concept to a great city and global population. It is not referring to the physical location or seat of the harlot. Rather, it is an indication that the city of the harlot will be global and powerful. Its center will have a commanding location. A city built adjacent to a major waterway would be well situated for commerce and as a center of government.

The ancient city of Babylon was located on in Mesopotamia on the Euphrates River, a major waterway. The location of historical Babylon, and the forthcoming location for the new Babylon, the harlot city, projects controlling power and wealth.

Indeed, Babylon will have an abundance of wealth and power. Jewelry, clothing, and other conspicuous aspects of wealth were abundant and flaunted. In addition to wealth and its trappings, the Babylonians pursued sexual pleasure, wine, and other forms of sensual gratification. Their relentless pursuit and adoration of earthly pleasures defied the Lord God.

The kings of the earth are portrayed as engaging in sexual immorality with the prostitute and being drunk with wine. The kings are not necessarily intoxicated debauchers. They clearly are inebriated with the new cult and their power. Both will be short-lived. The scope of this frightening and vivid vision is clearly global. The new world vision will be based on evil, immorality, and corruption. Thus, the entire world system is what is being foretold and judged by the angel in John's vision.

In Revelation 17:3, John was carried away in Spirit to a place in the wilds, where he saw a woman on a scarlet beast, "full of blasphemous names, and it had seven heads and ten horns." The seven heads are mountains on which the woman sits. They represent seven kings or kingdoms. Five of the seven have already collapsed: Egypt, Assyria, Babylon, Medo-Persia, and Greece. The sixth is Rome, the prominent kingdom of the first century. The last kingdom is to come, and it will be the short-lived Antichrist's kingdom. The ten horns are the ten kings that will assist the Antichrist with the rule of his kingdom. It will be built upon a one-world government, economy, and religion. A one-world government is the goal of many current nations and politicians today, and it is against the will of God, as we learn from the history of Babel.

The woman was a harlot. Her description of having seven heads and ten horns is the same as that of the Antichrist. She was wearing the regal colors of scarlet and purple. She was sitting on a scarlet beast—which is the Antichrist. A false religion will merge with and serve a false government. The Harlot is named "Babylon the great, mother of prostitutes and of the earth's abominations." She is the mother, the madam, of all religious prostitutes which are the world's false religions. "On her forehead was written a name of mystery: 'Babylon the great, mother of prostitutes and of earth's abominations.'" (Revelation 17:5). She is also called the harlot. The characterization "harlot" symbolizes idolatry in the Old Testament (Judges 2:17; 8:27, 33; Ezekiel 16:30–31, 36).

Dr. Robert Jeffress argues convincingly that this mother of all religious prostitutes is contrary to God's will in many regards, including its determination of the unification of all false religions into one religion.

"The problem with this idea is that it is contrary to the will of God. God is the one who created distinct nations with distinct boundaries and distinct ideas. He told the people to form the nations of the earth (Genesis 9:7). But the people of Babel said, "come, let us build for ourselves a city, and a tower whose top will reach into the heaven, and let us make for ourselves a name, otherwise we will be scattered abroad over the face of the whole earth" (Genesis 11:4). They built a tower to reach into the heavens and created their own religious system to worship the god of their imagination rather than the God of the Bible. This spirit of "Babylonianism" has infected the world ever since. Satan doesn't care what you believe, as long as you don't believe in Jesus Christ of the Bible – this is the spirit of "Babylonianism". Today it is called pluralism, inclusivism, or tolerance – the idea that there are many ways to God – and it will find its climax in this religious prostitute called "Babylon the great". I think this false religious system will probably be one-part evangelical Christianity, one part Catholicism, one part Islam, one-part New Age movement, and one-part positive thinking. This religious concoction will be so inclusive that it will offend nobody and attract everybody. That's the only way it can work." (Jeffress, p. 250-251).

"And I saw the woman drunk with the blood of the saints, the blood of the martyrs of Jesus." (Revelation 17:6). There will be many saints "born" during the Great Tribulation who come to Christ and die for Him rather than denying the Lord our God.

The harlot will be the final false religion over the earth. She is a metaphor for every false religion, religious apostasy, and the practice of idolatry. For a period of time, the harlot will have global authority and power. The world will commit to the Babylonian protocols and the practice of false worship. She will possess the hearts and souls of the unredeemed. The beast and the harlot will coexist until the time when the beast is ready to seize all power.

The woman drinking the blood of the saints predicts that the Antichrist will persecute all the believers in Jesus who will come to Christ during the Great Tribulation.

> "The important point is that false religion, represented here by the harlot, is a murderer. While the world becomes drunk with lust for her, the harlot becomes drunk with the blood of God's people. The vision was so appalling that when John saw her, he "wondered greatly," expressing that he was confused, shocked, astonished, and frightened by the ghastly vision of such a magnificent figure of a woman with such a deadly intent." MacArthur p. 265.

In 17-8, the angel says

> "The beast that you saw was, and is not, and is about to rise from the bottomless pit and go to destruction. And the dwellers on earth whose names have not been written in the book of life from the foundation of the world will marvel to see the beast, because it was and is not and is to come."

In verses 13:12–14, we learn that the beast had a mortal wound that was healed and that the beast will rise from the bottomless pit and will go to its destruction. This is a profoundly important statement. It means nothing less than that the beast's present powers to persecute believers will not last much longer. The near-term future for believers will be excessively violent. The pain and suffering will end with the capture and eternal punishing confinement of the beast found in verse 19:19–20. The beast's attack on believers has not yet started; once it does start, it will be short-lived. The time is drawing closer. We can anticipate its beginning in the escalating degradation of society and the rapidly increasing weaponization, conflicts, crime, and depravity that we are experiencing globally.

The seven heads of 17:9 are seven mountains. A woman sits on the seven mountains. This is a metaphor for the centers of seven governments or kingdoms. In Jeremiah and Daniel, this metaphor is developed. The mountain is a metaphor for a seemingly invincible and dominating force of governmental power. However, it is a power that is easily crushed and destroyed by God. The seven mountains are the seven kings of verse ten and are the world's empires. Five of the seven had already fallen at the time of the writing of Revelation. One, Rome, was still powerful. The seventh is still in our future. It will be the Antichrist's kingdom, and it will last for but a short while.

The harlot is powerful and sits over the kings and their kingdoms.

> "I will repay Babylon and all the inhabitants of Chaldea before your very eyes for all the evil that they have done in Zion, declares the Lord. Behold, I am against you O destroying mountain, declares the Lord, which destroys the whole earth; I will stretch out my hand against you, and roll you down from the crags, and male you a burnt mountain." (Jeremiah: 51-24-25)

"Then the iron, the clay, the bronze, the silver, and the gold, all together were broken in pieces and became like the chaff of the summer threshing flours; and the wind carried them away, so that not a trace of them could be found. But the stone that struck the image became a great mountain and filled the whole earth." (Daniel 2:35)…" And in the days of those kings the God of heaven will set up a kingdom that shall never be destroyed, nor shall the kingdom be left to other people. It shall break into pieces all these kingdoms and bring them to an end, and it shall stand forever, just as you saw that a stone was cut from a mountain by no human hand, and that it broke into pieces the iron, the bronze, the clay, the silver, and the gold. A great God has made know to the king what shall be after this. The dream is certain, and its interpretation sure." (Daniel 2:44-45).

At the time of the Revelation to John, Rome was the world's most powerful kingdom. Five empires had already vanished or collapsed: Egypt, Assyria, Babylon, Medo-Persia, and Greece. The remaining of the seven will be the Antichrist's kingdom, and it will survive for but a short while.

In Revelation 17:12, the angel explains that the ten kings of the ten kingdoms are the ten horns. The ten kings will become known when they receive their kingdoms from the Antichrist. They and their kingdoms will be under his rule. "They have not yet received royal power, but they are to receive authority as kings for one hour, together with the beast". (Revelation 17:12). The ten kings are a metaphor for the kings of the earth. They will be deceived by the beast, who will gather them up for a final, brief insurrection against the Lamb. While "one hour" may be a figurative timeframe, the Antichrist and his army will be swiftly crushed by the Lord Jesus Christ and His army in the final battle of Armageddon. The Antichrist and his army, the forces of evil and darkness, will never be able to defeat the "Lord of lords and King of kings".

> "[6]since indeed God considers it just to repay with affliction those who afflict you,[7]and to grant relief to you who are afflicted as well as to us, when the Lord Jesus is revealed from heaven with his mighty angels [8]in flaming fire, inflicting vengeance on those who do not know God and on those who do not obey the gospel of our Lord Jesus.[9]They will suffer the punishment of eternal destruction, away from the presence of the Lord and from the glory of his might". (2 Thessalonians 1:6-9).

God's Word is clear: Christ will crush the beast and his army.

The brief but terrifying and godless time of the Antichrist will be a time of a one-world government, economy, and religion. We are already seeing moves toward a one-world government. Globalism is a strong political movement in the United States, Europe, and elsewhere. We have international organizations like the World Bank, World Health Organization, United Nations, and even the World Council of Churches.

When the Antichrist has amassed his full power, the godless will "make war on the Lamb" (Revelation 17:14). The Lamb will conquer the Antichrist and destroy the reprobate along with him. The angel tells John the fate of the harlot and how the beast will come to hate her. Once he no longer has use for her, the Antichrist will also crush and destroy the harlot.

The angel then explains to John that the waters he saw:

"The waters that you saw, where the prostitute is seated, are peoples and multitudes and nations and languages. And the ten horns that you saw, they and the beast will hate the prostitute. They will make her desolate and naked and devour her flesh and burn her up with fire, for God has put into their hearts to carry out his purpose by being of one mind and handing over their royal power to the beast, until the words of God are fulfilled. And the woman you say is the great city that has dominion over the kings of earth." (Revelation 17:15-18).

At this time, and according to God's plan, the Antichrist now has all the power he thinks he needs to launch the next phase of his master plan. He will no longer have use for the false religious system and the church that he used to gain control over the world. He will destroy them with the help of the ten kings. The Antichrist will then become the unchallenged global dictator, worshiped by the kingdoms and empires of the world. It is his ultimate objective to be the sole focus of the world's worship.

The "beast and the ten horns will make the harlot "desolate and naked". They will devour her flesh and burn her up with fire." (17:16). The beast and his army will eliminate the prostitute. The economic system will collapse. This will be a parallel to the judgment that God pronounced on Israel.

[39]And I will give you into their hands, and they shall throw down your vaulted chamber and break down your lofty places. They shall strip you of your clothes and take y our beautiful jewels and leave you naked and

bare. [40]They shall bring up a crowd against you, and they shall stone you and cut you to pieces with their swords. [41]And they shall burn your houses and execute judgments upon you in the sight of many women. I will make you stop playing the whore, and you shall also give payment mop more." (Ezekiel: 16:39-41)

The one-world government pursued in our current times will finally come to be in this prophecy. However, all will change quickly and decisively when Jesus returns in all glory and power.

We are called to always remember, in the midst of our troubles and the evil of today, that God is in charge. God is the Great Architect of everything. He is the Architect of the end of times. Everything that happens is according to His divine plan. We must also remember that false religions have existed since the fall of man in the Garden. The Christian must always be discerning and faithful to the one true Word.

In reflecting on the Revelation of John, believers need to remember that they will not be present on earth when the times of cleansing and terror arrive. In His limitless love, Jesus Christ, the Messiah, will have already raptured His Church, raising the millions upon millions of believers to the clouds of heaven before all of the tribulations begin. The Great Tribulation of seven years, and the subsequent return of Jesus to earth, will mark the time when Christ will destroy all evil. This time will be followed by the creation of a new heaven and a new earth. Christ will work with the Jews for their conversion to Christianity before, and in particular after, the Great Tribulation ends. Following the Great

Tribulation, Christ will achieve a massive conversion to Christianity in the millennial kingdom on earth, which will begin after the Great Tribulation and the Battle of Armageddon.

Please see *The Gift of Salvation* by Dennis Richard Mahoney, available at Amazon.com and bookstores.

Chapter 20

The Fall of Babylon

The Fall of Babylon

18 After this I saw another angel coming down from heaven, having great authority, and the earth was made bright with his glory. ^{2}And he called out with a mighty voice,
"^{2}Fallen, fallen is Babylon the great! She has become a dwelling place for demons, a haunt for every unclean spirit a haunt for every unclean bird, a haunt for every unclean and detestable beast ^{3}For all nations have drunk the wine of passion of her sexual immorality and the kings of the earth have committed immorality with her, and the merchants of the earth have grown rich from the power of her luxurious living." ^{4}Then I heard another voice from heaven saying, "Come out of her, my people, lest you take part in her sins, lest you share in her plagues; for her sins are heaped high as heaven, and God has remembered her iniquities. ^{6}Pay her back as she herself has paid back others, and repay her double for her deeds; mix a double portion for her in the cup she mixed. ^{7}As she has glorified herself in luxury, so give her a like measure of torment and mourning, since in her heart she says, 'I sit as a queen, I am no widow, and morning I shall never see'. ^{8}For this reason her plagues will come in a single day, Death and mourning and famine, and she will burn up with fire; for mighty is the Lord God who has judged her." ^{9}And the kings of the earth, who committed sexual immorality and lived in luxury with her, will weep and wail over her when they see the smoke of her burning. ^{10}They will stand far off, in fear of her torment, and say, "Alas! Alas! You great

city, you mighty city, Babylon! For in a single hour your judgment has come."

[11]And the merchants of the earth weep and mourn for her, since no one buys their cargo anymore, [12]cargo of gold, silver, jewels, pearls, fine linen, purple cloth, silk, scarlet cloth, all kinds of scented wood, all kinds of articles of ivory, all kinds of articles of costly wood, bronze, iron, and marble, [13]cinnamon, spice, incense, myrrh, frankincense, wine, oil, fine flour, wheat, cattle and sheep, horses, and chariots, and slaves, that is, human souls.
[14]"The fruit for which your soul longed has gone from you and all your delicacies and your splendors are lost to you never to be found again!" [15]The merchants of these wares, who gained wealth from her, will stand far off, in fear of her torment, weeping and mourning aloud, [16]Alas, alas, for the great city that was clothed in fine linen in purple and scarlet, adorned with gold, with jewels, and with pearls! [17]For in a single hour all this wealth has been laid waste. And all the shipmasters and seafaring men, sailors and all whose trade is on the sea, stood far off [18]and cried out as they saw the smoke of her burning. "What city was like the great city?

[19]And they threw dust on their heads as they wept and mourned, crying out, "Alas, alas, for the great city where all who had ships at sea grew rich by her wealth! For in a single hour she has been laid waste. [20]Rejoice over her, O heaven, and you saints and apostles and prophets for God has given judgement for you against her!" [21]Then a mighty angel took up a stone like a great

millstone and threw it into the sea, saying, "So will Babylon the great city be thrown down by violence, and will be found no more; [22]and the sound of harpists and musicians, of flute players and trumpeters, will be heard in you no more and a craftsman of any craft will be found in you no more, and the sound of the mill will be heard in you no more [23]and the light of a lamp will shine in you no more, and the voice of bridegroom and bride will be heard in you no more, for your merchants were the great ones of the earth, and all nations were deceived by your sorcery.[24] And in her was found the blood of prophets and of saints, and of all who have been slain on earth."

In Revelation 18:1, another angel comes down from heaven, who is of "great authority", so much so that the "earth was made bright by his glory". This angel reiterates the proclamation made in 14:8 by the "second angel's" proclamation that "Fallen, fallen is Babylon the great". In approximately 725 B.C., Isaiah 21:9 prophesied, "Fallen, fallen is Babylon; and all the carved images of her gods he has shattered to the ground." We see Isaiah's prophecy again some 825 years later in the revelation that John received on Patmos.

In Revelation 18:2, this angel tells John in a "mighty" voice of the coming collapse of the Antichrist and his kingdom, marking the fall of "Babylon the great". The word fallen repeats twice as: "Fallen, fallen is Babylon the great!" (Revelation 18:2). Babylon will be turned into a great wilderness, as seen by John in this vision. The repetition of "fallen" could be for emphasis because this prophecy is so significant. The financial system of the beast appeared so strong, even unbreakable, but it will completely collapse.

Additionally, this revelation occurs immediately after John learns from the angel of the seven bowls in Revelation 17:1 of the "judgment of the great prostitute" and the collapse of the beast's religious system. The fall of Babylon the great will be fast and complete. Babylon was filthy: she had "drunk with the wine of the passion of her sexual immorality, and the kings of the earth have committed immorality with her, and the merchants of the earth have grown rich". (Revelation 18:3).

Babylon ignored warnings that included the 144,000 Jewish evangelists, the two witnesses, and the angel from the heavens who proclaimed the gospel and called for repentance. The Antichrist's empire will be crushed by the Lord's invincible power.

John then heard a new voice coming from heaven. This voice is the voice of God. It is a call to "come out of her, my people, lest you take part in her sins, lest you share in her plagues." (Revelation 18:4). The morally bankrupt people could yet be saved from God's wrath that is coming. The call to come out of sinful cultures is relevant today and was relevant to the churches in Thyatira and Laodicea. God's message is that punishment will come quickly and "she will burn with fire" for God "has judged her." (Revelation 18:8). We learn that although most will be punished for eternity after Christ delivers His judgment and makes war on the Antichrist and Satan, those who come to Christ during the Great Tribulation will be saved. The saved will include the tribulation martyrs. Dr. Robert Jeffress gives us a compelling description of sin:

> "In Revelation 18:5, John said that Babylon's sins "have piled up as high as heaven, and God has remembered her iniquities." This is an allusion to Genesis 11, the city of Babel. The people of Babel built that tower to

heaven brick upon brick as a sign of their rebellion against the true God. That's the way sin is: we put sin upon sin until we build a wall of separation between God and us." ("Final Conquest", Dr. Robert Jeffress, Pathway to Victory, 2020, p.261).

The Mosaic Law of "eye for eye, tooth for tooth, hand for hand, foot for foot, burn for burn, wound for wound, stripe for stripe" (Exodus 21:24) is the message of Revelation 18:6. In God's time, sin brings punishment. The Babylonians will be punished according to their sins. There will be plagues, great torment, and mourning. Her "sins are heaped high as heaven," and she will be paid "back as she herself has paid back others, and repay her double for her deeds; mix a double portion for her in the cup she mixed." (Revelation 18:5–6). The double portion from her own cup is just retribution from the Lord God. It is retribution for the saints' blood that Babylon shed. Kings and merchants who lived in immorality wept and wailed at the destruction of their riches in the fire thrown down by God. The merchant class committed many sins in accumulating great wealth and riches in their sinful economy. Babylon's destruction will occur in a single hour.

A plea is made in Revelation 18:7 that God's punishments correspond to the seriousness of the sin in the words, "so give her a like measure of torment and mourning". God will deliver justice. He will enact His justice in a single day: "For this reason her plagues will come in a single day, Death and mourning and famine, and she will be burned up with fire; for mighty is the Lord God who has judged her." (Revelation 18:8). The sinners mourned as they watched the flames and the continual smoke that rises up forever and ever. Smoke, when recorded in Scripture, indicates that God's judgment is irreversible.

"But first I will double repay their iniquity and their sin, because they have polluted my land with heir carcasses of their detestable idols, and have filled my inheritance with their abominations." (Jeremiah 16:18).

Mosaic Law was well documented in the Old Testament. One clear example of its fulfillment is found in the Book of Daniel, which chronicles the history of the ancient city of Babylon and its King Belshazzar, whose kingdom was divided when God found it morally deficient.

[25] And this is the writing that was inscribed: Mene, Mene, Tekel, and Parsin. [26]This is the interpretation of the matter: Mene, God has numbered the days of your kingdom and brought it to an end. [27]Tekel you have been weighed in the balances and found wanting; [28]Peres, your kingdom is divided and given to Medes and Persians. [29]Then Belshazzar gave the command…[30]then that very night, Belshazzar the Chaldean kind was killed…and his kingdom was divided."
(Daniel 5, 25:30).

Babylon held to the delusion that its wealth would give her security. In Revelation 3:17, it is recorded that the church at Laodicea had a false sense of security in its wealth when, in reality, it was "wretched, pitiable, poor, blind, and naked" for essentially worshiping the false god of materialism. It will be too late for the merchants, kings, and mariners of Babylon. We read in 18:9 that the "great city's" time has come. The Lord's patience has come to its end.

The beast held its power with a corrupt government, and the prostitute maintained her grip on the economy through a corrupt financial system. We read in Revelation 18:11–17 of this abominable domination. They will grieve and wail aloud over their loss of commercial wares and "fine clothing in linen, purple, scarlet, gold, jewels, and pearls." (Revelation 18:16). The merchants, shipmasters, and seamen will all be laid to financial waste. They will be stripped of all wealth and power.

The destruction of "Babylon the great" will be mourned by three groups who will be crushed in its economic collapse. These three groups include kings, shipmasters and their passengers, and merchants of all types—each devastated in a single hour. Essentially, no one will be spared. God's judgment will be swiftly meted out. Babylon will be judged by God in one hour: "For in a single hour all this wealth has been laid waste." (Revelation 18:17).

Stripped of their riches and their ability to continue their trades and businesses, the people of Babylon the great will mourn and weep aloud. The financial empire and system of the Antichrist will be destroyed in a moment. He and the merchants and profiteers from his financial system will watch his empire literally burn. The destruction will be complete. While the devastated merchants and their cohorts lament, the saints, apostles, and prophets in heaven will rejoice in God's deliverance of justice (Revelation 18:20–22). Babylon's sins included the murder of prophets, saints, and believers, whose blood was found in the ashes. (Revelation 18:24).

The prophet Jeremiah cast a rock and a scroll into the Euphrates River to illustrate that Babylon will sink and not rise again (Jeremiah 51:63–64). We see this demonstration again in Revelation 18:21, when a "mighty angel took up a stone like a great millstone and threw it into the sea". The great millstone "will be found no more." Nor will the sounds of life—the voice of the bridegroom and bride—be heard anymore.

Revelation 18:24 ends with, "And in her was found the blood of prophets and of saints, and of all who have been slain on earth." With this complete fall of Babylon and the defeat of the beast, the Lord will have repaid the blood of His martyrs. The martyrs, the prophets, and the saints lost their lives because of their faithfulness. They will be rewarded as saints who will eternally sing songs of praise in heaven.

Greed is the core of Babylon's failures and sins. Babylon oppressed believers. The saints and the believers are justified and will be oppressed no more. God acts in His own time—but God does act. He did not destroy the tower of Babel immediately. The Lord is merciful in His patience. In His mercy, He gives repentant sinners time to reform.

Chapter 21

Rejoicing in Heaven

Rejoicing in Heaven

19 After this I heard what seemed to be the loud voice of a great multitude in heaven crying out,

"Hallelujah! Salvation and glory and power belong to our God, [2]for his judgments are true and just; for he has judged the great prostitute who corrupted the earth with her immorality and has avenged on her the blood of his servants. [3]Once more they cried out "Hallelujah! The smoke from her goes up forever and ever."
[4]And the twenty-four elders and the four living creatures fell down and worshiped God who was seated on the throne, saying, "Amen. Hallelujah!" [5]And from the throne came a voice saying, "Praise our God all you his servants, you who fear him, small and great."

The Marriage Supper of the Lamb.

[6]Then I heard what seemed to be the voice of a great multitude, like the roar of many waters and like the sound of mighty peals of thunder, crying out, "Hallelujah! For the Lord our God the Almighty reigns let us rejoice and exult and give him the glory, for the marriage of the Lamb has come, and his Bride has made herself ready; [8] it was granted her to clothe herself with fine linen, bright and pure" for the fine linen is the righteous deeds of the saints. [9]And the angel said to me, "Write this: Blessed are those who are invited to the

marriage supper of the Lamb." And he said to me, "These are the true words of God." [10]Then I fell down at his feet to worship him, but he said to me, "You must not do that! I am a fellow servant with you and your brothers who hold to the testimony of Jesus. Worship God." For the testimony of Jesus is the spirit of prophecy.

In Revelation 19, the victory of the Lord of lords and King of kings will unfold. It tells of the Parousia, or Second Coming of Christ, as promised in Scripture. Christ's return to earth is a certainty. There are 1,800 references to Jesus Christ's second coming in the Old Testament, and the New Testament contains over 300 such references.

At His second coming, Christ will judge the unbelievers for their sins and wickedness. He will terminate Satan's dominion and banish him to the Lake of Fire, which is hell. He will judge the living and the dead not already raptured or otherwise in heaven. Christ will also avenge the persecution of His people. In short, Christ will return to earth to reestablish God's kingdom on earth.

The saints in heaven will rejoice at the reestablishment of God's earthly kingdom. The wailing on earth will be replaced by joy in the heavens. The saints will cry out in gratitude for God's saving grace. They will also rejoice over God's banishment of sinners from the earth and His creation of a new earth and the Millennial Kingdom. Christ's return will be glorious, swift, and all-powerful.

"Hallelujah" translates from the Hebrew combination meaning "to praise" and "God". This combination was carried into Greek as "Hallelujah". It is often sung in praise of God's glory (Psalms 113–118). Hallelujah is also a praise to God for His judgment of the wicked who oppress His people (Psalm 104:35).

Four cries of "Hallelujah!" are heard from heaven. "Hallelujah" translates from Hebrew as "Praise be to God." The first song of Hallelujah sings praise that the great harlot is fallen.

The saints call out, "Hallelujah! Salvation and glory and power belong to our God, for his judgments are true and just." (Revelation 19:1). The rejoicing is for God's judgment of Babylon's religious platform, which is based on the beast and the great harlot. The great harlot is the false church that will thrive during the first half of the seven-year Great Tribulation. The great harlot will be an instrumental component of the earthly rise of the Antichrist. When God judges and destroys the great harlot's "church", the rejoicing of the saints in heaven will begin at her fall. At the halfway mark of the Great Tribulation, the Antichrist and the ten kings will decide they are finished with the great harlot and will destroy her. The saints in heaven will rejoice at this sign that the Lord's Day is coming.

The second cry of "Hallelujah!" will occur when Babylon's economic system is judged and destroyed. The great city will then be fully consumed. "Hallelujah! The smoke from her goes up forever and ever," (Revelation 19:3), symbolizing

God's irreversible judgment, just as the millstone was cast into the sea. The ashes of Babylon will continue to smolder, symbolizing that it was completely destroyed and its punishment is for eternity.

The third cry of "Hallelujah!" is sung by a different choir—the twenty-four elders and the four living creatures who fell down before the throne of God continue the singing. "From the throne came a voice saying, 'Amen. Hallelujah! Praise our God, all you his servants, you who fear him, small and great!'" (Revelation 19:4). God's servants rejoice that He sits on His throne forever. The Lord has triumphed over evil—and always will.

Next comes the fourth cry of "Hallelujah," sung by the voices of a great multitude, with a sound "like the roar of many waters and like the sound of mighty peals of thunder, crying out, 'Hallelujah! For the Lord our God the Almighty reigns.'" (Revelation 19:6). The multitude's praises of God for His majesty and sovereignty dwarf any earthly chorus. Those invited to the marriage supper of the Lamb are the believers who are members of Christ's church (Matthew 22:1–14; 25:10; 26:29). The Lord's reign will have no rival or challenge. The last song heard is the song of praise: "For the marriage of the Lamb has come, and His bride, the church, has made herself ready… with fine linen, bright and pure" (Revelation 19:6–8).

> "Husbands, love your wives, as Christ loved the church and gave himself up for her, that he might sanctify her, having cleansed her by washing of water with the word,

so that he might present the church to himself in splendor, without spot or wrinkle or any such thing, that she might be holy and without blemish." (Ephesians 5:25-27).

Christ paid a dowry, and a "wedding contract" was executed when He shed His blood on the cross. Christ will come again in the clouds above us to rapture His church, sparing believers from the suffering of the seven-year Great Tribulation, immediately before what will be a cleansing of the earth begins. Christ will return to the earth with His church following the Great Tribulation to wage the final battle at Armageddon. Christ, with His army, will defeat evil forever in this battle, which will last just one hour. Following Christ's victory on earth, the millennial kingdom of 1,000 years will begin. These prophecies and promises of the Lord align perfectly with the Jewish wedding prerequisites of a marriage contract and dowry payment, a marriage ceremony in the groom's home, and a wedding feast. The wedding guests at the Lord's wedding to His church will likely be the Old Testament saints, tribulation martyrs, and the New Testament believers—His church.

Scripture tells us that the bride is ready for the Groom. She was made ready by the forgiving grace of God the Father. Working through His Holy Spirit, God will purge all sin and imperfection from His Bride so that His church will become as a virgin without blame. The bride of Christ will wear a wedding gown woven by the Lord. It is to be the Groom's gift of righteousness and grace.

"I will greatly rejoice in the Lord, my soul; shall exult in mt God, for he has clothed me with the garments of salvation; he has covered me with the robe of righteousness, as a bridegroom decks himself like a priest with a beautiful head-dress, as a bride adorns herself with her jewels." (Isaiah 61:10).

Before the wedding can proceed, the enemies of the groom must be converted or eliminated. Thus, Christ will not return to the earth until the end of the Great Tribulation can accomplish this cleansing. The Parousia, or the second coming of Jesus, will occur exactly seven years after His rapture of His church to heaven. The first three and one-half years of the Tribulation will see the initial and temporary rise of the Antichrist and his false religion, and the second three and one-half years will see their destruction and the destruction of all evil in God's kingdom.

Blessed days are coming and will remain for eternity.

The Rider on a White Horse

[11]Then I saw heaven opened, and behold, a white horse! The one sitting on it is called Faithful and True, and in righteousness he judges and makes war. [12] His eyes are like a flame of fire, and on his head are many diadems, and he has a name written that no one knows but himself. [13]He is clothed in a robe dipped in blood, and the name by which he is called is The Word of God. [14]And the armies of heaven arrayed in fine linen white and pure, were following him on white horses. [15]From his mouth comes a sharp sword with which to strike down the nations, and he will rule them with a rod of

iron. He will tread the winepress of the fury of the wrath of God the Almighty. [16]On his robe and on his thigh he has a name written, King of kings and Lord of lords.

[17]Then I saw an angel standing in the sun, and with a loud voice he called to all the birds that fly directly overhead. "Come, gather for the great supper of God, [18] to eat the flesh of kings, the flesh of captains, the flesh of horses, and their riders, and the flesh of all men, both free and slave, both small and great. [19]And I saw the beast and the kings of the earth with their armies gathered to make war against his army. [20]And the beast was captured, and with it the false prophet who in its presence had done the signs by which he deceived those who had received the mark of the beast and those who worshiped its image. These two were thrown alive into the lake of fire that burns with sulfur. [21]And the rest were slain by the sword that came from the mouth of him who was sitting on the horse, and all the birds were gorged with their flesh.

Revelation 19:11 unveils the greatest promise of all time, the return of Jesus Christ, our Lord and Savior, who will reign forever on earth. Christ and His armies will defeat and forever destroy the beast, the false prophet, and their armies. Before Jesus can begin the wedding feast, He must, and He will, return to the earth with His bride.

Faithful and True identifies the rider on the white horse as Jesus. See Revelation 1:5 (Jesus Christ, the faithful witness), and Revelation 3:14 (Amen, the faithful and true witness, the beginning of God's creation). White is the color of victory. Jesus will be returning to an earth still populated by sinners and the Antichrist, who had been persecuting Israel and believers. Those still alive were suffering from the ravages of martyrdom, the wicked cruelty of the Antichrist, and God's punishing judgments that befell the earth. Soon, all will be settled.

Believers must remember and take comfort that Christ will come down to the clouds over the earth and there meet with His church—composed of all believers, living and dead—and rapture them to heaven. Christ will literally lift them up to heaven. Please see the author's prior work, The Gift of Salvation, for a biblical proof of the Pretribulational Rapture.

The kings of the earth will decide to join forces to destroy the Antichrist in the valley of Armageddon. As the battle begins, the earthly warrior kings will look up to the sky and see our Lord and Savior, Jesus the Christ. The kings' armies then choose to unite together to fight Jesus Christ.

John then sees heaven open, and a white horse and He who sat on it appear. "Then I saw heaven opened, and behold, a white horse! The one sitting on it is called Faithful and True, and in righteousness He judges and makes war." (Revelation 19:11). He is called The Word of God. He will be followed by the armies of heaven, who are His church. Christ's army will also ride on white horses and will wear fine white linen. The fine linen worn by the armies of heaven identifies them as the bride of the Lamb. Jesus the Christ, the King of kings, will have eyes of blazing fire, for He is the fierce warrior. His head will be adorned with diadems, which are regal crowns displaying His power and authority to rule. His blazing eyes symbolize His coming judgment. His vestments will be blood-soaked with the blood of His enemies. His name is written on His robes as "King of kings and Lord of lords." Jesus, once the infant Child who was humbled as a man, now rides on His white horse with His army in His full glory and might.

We read in Luke 10:22 that Jesus said to His disciples, "All things have been handed over to me by my Father, and no one knows who the Son is except the Father, or who the Father is except the Son and anyone to whom the Son chooses to reveal Him." Christ is the King of kings and Lord of lords, who is named The Word of God. He also has a name that no one but Himself knows. It is a divine mystery that veils the full nature of Jesus. He is coming to strike down the wicked and will tread the winepress of God's wrath, and His robes will be spotted with the blood of the wicked.

> "I have trodden the winepress alone, and from the peoples no one was with me; I trod them in my anger and trampled them in my wrath; their lifeblood spattered on my garments, and stained my apparel." (Isaiah 63:3)

The battle will be swift. Our Lord Jesus Christ will crush the grapes of wrath, and red blood will flow. "From His mouth comes a sharp sword with which to strike down nations, and He will rule them with a rod of iron." (Revelation 19:15). The beast will be quickly seized by the Lord's armies. The Lord will stand on the Mount of Olives, and it shall be split in two (Zechariah 14:3-4). The Lord will banish forever the beast and the false prophet. He "threw them alive into the lake of fire that burns with sulfur" (Revelation 19:20), whereas their soldiers will be merely killed in battle.

Revelation gives a powerful juxtaposition. The marriage supper of the Lamb (verse 9) presents the true words of God that all believers are the wedding brides of the Lord. In contrast, the "great supper of God" (verse 17) describes, in stark contrast, the fierce judgment of the beast and unrepentant sinners. The faithful will all be saved. The demonic and unsaved will come to a horrific end. Vultures and birds of prey will "eat the flesh of kings, the flesh of captains, the flesh of mighty men, and the flesh of horses and their riders" (Revelation 19:18). The time will come for Christ to make war on sin. "And the rest were slain by the sword that came from the mouth of Him who was sitting on the horse, and all the birds were gorged with their flesh." (Revelation 19:21). So many died that day that even the birds called to the great supper of God by His angel could not finish devouring the dead. It took men seven months to bury all of the bodies.

Significantly, the angel's invitation to the birds to eat the flesh of the kings is a remembrance of Old Testament covenant curses and the Lord's condemnation of Gog and Magog.

> But on that day, the day that Gog shall come against the land of Israel, declares the Lord God, my wrath will be roused in my anger. (Ezekiel 38:18).

> And your dead body shall be food for all birds of the air and for the beasts of the earth, and there shall be no one to frighten them away. (Deuteronomy 28:26).

The beast and its false prophet were captured and thrown alive into the lake of fire. The sharp sword that protruded from the mouth of Faithful and True, from the very mouth of Jesus the Christ, struck down the wicked. The carnage was complete. The beast, the false prophet, and the great prostitute we read of earlier represent corrupt, sinful institutions, not single individuals. Christ will come to defeat sin and all forces of evil. His victory shall be complete.

It is undeniable that the Bible is one continuous revelation of the truth, of the Word of God. The Bible tells us exactly what has been, what is now, and what will come to pass.

God is patient. He has waited since the beginning of time. He has already waited two thousand years after the crucifixion of His Son. He wants our repentance and faithfulness and gives us every chance to respond. God is very forgiving. However, when His patience has run its course, His wrath will be crushing. The great truth is that pleasing God brings us great joy on earth and eternal life hereafter. The prophets were given their messages by Almighty God. They passed on these looks into the future as God willed for our instruction and benefit. Continuously through history, God has instructed, guided, warned, and blessed us. He gave us thousands upon thousands of years since the original sin in the garden to follow His will. Only at the end of times will unrepentant sinners and Satan's armies be forever punished. The rest of us will know joy without limit.

God is always faithful. These passages depict the fulfillment of God's greatest promise and gift to His creation. Christ will never forget or forsake His church. He will reign with His church in peace and glory.

"The Bible clearly teaches that we enter this world alienated from God. We are like prisoners on Death row awaiting our execution. Jesus Christ came the first time to be our Saviour – to pardon us from our sins if we accept His forgiveness. But if we leave this world without receiving that pardon from our sins, then we will face Jesus one day as our Judge. The second coming of Jesus Christ will be the worst day of your life if you have to face Him as your Judge. But the second coming of Jesus Christ will be the best day of your life if you receive His forgiveness now and look forward to the great future He has planned for you."
("Final Conquest", Dr. Robert Jeffress, Path to Victory, 2020, p.284)

Chapter 22

The Thousand Years

The Thousand Years

20 Then I saw an angel coming down from heaven, holding in his hand the key to the bottomless pit and a great chain. ²And he seized the dragon, that ancient serpent, who is the devil and Satan, and bound him for a thousand years, ³and threw him into the pit, and shut it and sealed it over him, so that he might not deceive nations any longer, until the thousand years were ended. After that he must be released for a little while.

⁴Then I saw thrones, and seated on them were those to whom the authority to judge was committed. Also, I saw the souls of those who had been beheaded for the testimony of Jesus and for the Word of God, and those who had not worshiped the beast or its image and had not received its mark on their foreheads or their hands. They came to life and reigned with Christ for a thousand years. ⁵The rest of the dead did not come to life until the thousand years were ended. This is the first resurrection. ⁶Blessed and holy is the one who shares in the first resurrection! Over such the second Death has no power, but they will be priests of God and of Christ, and they will reign with him for a thousand years.

Revelation 20:1-6 is the most debated passage of Revelation among theologians. As discussed separately (pp. x–y), the three major Millennial views are Premillennialism, Postmillennialism, and Amillennialism. Premillennialism is the only view consistent with a literal interpretation of Scripture. God has given us His Word so that we can believe, obey, and serve. Why would the Lord speak to us in riddle or metaphor?

Premillennialism incorporates the essential Pretribulational rapture of the church and a literal one-thousand-year period of Christ's reign on earth. Postmillennialism postulates that Christ will return to earth to reign after the gospel is spread throughout the world, transforming it. There is no indication that we are moving toward such events. Amillennialists believe that a non-literal interpretation is valid and that the one thousand years is the same as the current church age that we are in.

The dragon in 20:2 is the ancient serpent, Satan. The dragon will be thwarted by an angel sent from heaven. The dragon will be bound in chains and confined in a great pit for the one-thousand-year millennium. When the dragon is released, it will be to his final defeat. Satan will not be able to interrupt the one thousand golden years of peace, well-being, and righteousness of the millennium. Being chained and confined, Satan will not be able to deceive the world for one thousand years.

Those who died in Christ will come to life again to sit on the thrones of judgment to assist Christ in His millennial reign. The wicked, and those who died following a life of evil, will be called to life briefly at the end of times, when they will experience their second Death and will be cast into the lake of fire for eternity.

Postmillennialists and Amillennialists must interpret God's Word as He gives it to us in Scripture to find an alternate meaning, rather than accept the biblical Word.

The Defeat of Satan

[7] And when the thousand years are ended, Satan will be released from his prison [8]and will come out to deceive the nations that are at the four corners of the earth, Gog and Magog, to gather them for battle; their number is like the sand of the sea. [9]And they marched up over the broad plain of the earth and surrounded the camp of the saints and the beloved city, but fire came down from heaven and consumed them, [10]and the devil who had deceived them was thrown into the lake of fire and sulfur where the beast and the false prophet were, and they will be tormented day and night for ever and ever.

The dragon, the ancient serpent who is Satan himself, will now be dealt with. Satan will be freed briefly to deceive the people and wage his final battle. Satan will fight the armies of Gog and Magog. These are the same names of the oppressors of Israel of ancient times who were killed by fire from heaven (Ezekiel 39:1–6, 17–20; Revelation 19:17–18, 21). Satan's efforts will be thwarted. He will fail to destroy God's church. The Lord bound Satan with a great chain and threw him into the bottomless pit for one thousand years. God's containment of Satan symbolizes that the devil will be unable to harm or deceive believers or the nations at large during his imprisonment in the bottomless pit. This will occur just before the start of the millennium, the time of righteousness when Christ will rule on earth for one thousand years. It will be a time of global peace, which requires the lock-up of Satan. The words "bound, shut it, and sealed" convey the complete emasculation, or removal, of Satan, which is the only interpretation consistent with the golden age of the millennium.

We are currently living in the "church age". This period is given to us by God to allow non-Jews to become members of His Kingdom, in preparation for the rapture. We read in Romans that God will shift His focus back to Israel at the end of the church age, which will mark the timing of the rapture of believers.

> "[2]God has not rejected his people whom he foreknew. Do you not know what Scripture says of Elijah, how he appeals to God against Israel? [3]Lord, they have killed your prophets, they have demolished your altars, and I alone am left, and they seek my life." [4]But what is God's reply to him? "I have kept for myself seven thousand men who have not bowed to the knee of Baal. [5]So too at the present time there is a remnant, chosen by grace." (Romans 11:2-5).

> "Lest you be wise in your own sight, I do not want you to be unaware of this mystery brothers: a partial hardening has come upon Israel, until the fullness of the Gentiles has come in." (Romans 11:25).

God will focus on the Jews during the millennium, the one-thousand-year period following the Great Tribulation when Jesus Christ rules on earth. When every last savable Gentile has been saved, God will return His focus to the Jews. God promised a kingdom for the Jews at a future time. This great promise is known as the Davidic Covenant, which the Lord God made with David.

> "When your days are fulfilled and you lie down with your fathers, I will raise up your offspring after you,

who shall come from your body, and I will establish his kingdom. He shall build a house for my name, and I will establish the throne of his kingdom forever."
(2 Samuel 7:12-13)

"If his children forsake my law and do not walk according to my rules, if they violate my statutes and do not keep my commandments, then I will punish their transgression with the rod and their iniquity with stripes, but I will not remove from him my steadfast love or be false to my faithfulness. I will not violate my covenant or alter the word that went forth from my lips. Once for all I have sworn by my holiness; I will not lie to David. His offspring shall endure forever his throne as long as the sun before me. Like the moon it shall be established forever, a faithful witness in the skies. *Selah*."
(Psalm 89:30-37).

In His final moments on earth with His disciples, they asked Christ "Lord, will you at this time restore the kingdom to Israel?" (Acts 1:6). Christ responded:

"It is not for you to know the times or seasons that the Father has fixed by his own authority. But you will receive power when the Holy Spirit has come upon you, and you will be my witnesses in Jerusalem and in all Judea and Samaria and to the end of the earth. And when he had said these things, as they were looking on, he was lifted up, and a cloud took him out of their sight. And while they were gazing into heaven as he went, behold, two men stood by them in white robes, and said, "Men of Galilee, why do you stand looking into heaven? This Jesus, who was taken up from you into heaven, will come in the same way as you saw him go into heaven."
(Acts 1:6-11).

The great events to come, promised by Jesus the Christ, will be His rapture of believers, the Great Tribulation for the purification of worthy sinners and the eternal punishment of the wicked, and the millennial kingdom.

Theologians disagree on the key details of the one-thousand-year period, or the "millennium", articulated in Revelation 20. The three primary views of the millennium are Posttribulationism, Amillennialism, and Premillennialism. The essence of these interpretations are:

"Postmillennialism":
Through Christian influence, society will continue to improve until it reaches a utopian -like state. Thus, it is believers who will bring in the millennial kingdom. Christ will return after this general period of peace and prosperity has been established.

"Amillennialism":
The millennial kingdom is not a future, thousand-year kingdom on earth. Rather, it is a spiritual kingdom that refers to Christ's rule in the hearts of His people during the church age. Some Amillennialists believe the millennial kingdom is a literal kingdom in heaven, where Christ's saints rule with him. However, they reject the notion of a future, physical kingdom on earth.

"Premillennialism":
The millennial kingdom refers to a future, physical kingdom that Christ will establish at His return. The kingdom, which well be centered in Jerusalem, will last for one-thousand-years, after which this world will be

destroyed and replaced by the new earth. This view is the most natural way to understand Revelation 20-20.

(Because The Time is Near", John MacArthur, Moody Publishers, Chicago, 2007, p.296)

Postmillennialism seems to suggest that the world will keep improving and growing spiritually on its own such that creation can itself make the earth worthy of Christ's return. This belief seems unlikely. There is no discernable evidence that humankind is making the world better, safer, and more spiritual. "Christian Reconstructionism", or "Dominionism" are based on getting believers into leadership positions in society and government, making a better earth in the process. Christians spread the Gospel, but are not able to defeat evil and sin. That is the dominion of the Lord.

Amillennialism professes that when Israel rejected Jesus, God's promises were transferred over to the church. The Church will fulfill the millennial promises. There will be no earthly millennial kingdom. The promises made by God to Israel now rest with the church. Any binding or restriction of Satan will happen within ourselves and not in a dungeon. Challenging this position, sin appears to be continually increasing, not decreasing. This position is in contradiction with Scripture, such as Genesis 15:9-21, the Abrahamic covenant of God's unconditional promise to give his people the land of Israel forever.

As a Premillennialist and Pretribulationist, this author focuses on the Premillennial view in this book. For a comprehensive study and Biblical Proof of the Premillennial and Pretribulation views, please refer to "The Gift of Salvation" by this Author, Dennis Richard Mahoney available on Amazon Books.

Many theologians find it difficult to refute the primacy of Premillennialism. Adopting this position is a requirement of any endeavor to accept and believe Scripture as written, that is, pursuing a literal interpretation of the Bible. Jesus told us that *He* is coming back for us, which will encompass His triumphant defeat of Satan and peace on earth. John sees an angel "coming down from heaven, holding in his hand the keys to the bottomless pit and a great chain" (Revelation 20:1).

> "This angel will "seize the dragon, that ancient serpent, who is the devil and Satan, and bound him for a thousand years. And threw him into the pit, and shut it and sealed it over him, so that he might not deceive the nations any longer, until the thousand years were ended." (Revelation 20:2-3).

Only Premillennialism and its literal reading of Scripture are clearly and specifically consistent with Scripture. Noted theologians, including Floyd Hamilton, an Amillennialist, state that Premillennialism is the position that aligns with a literal reading of Scripture. A literal interpretation of Scripture is consistent with the belief that God desires that we understand His Word and command. Amillennialism is the position farthest away from Premillennialism. Floyd Hamilton writes:

> "Now we must frankly admit that a literal interpretation of the Old Testament Prophecies gives us just such a picture of an earthly reign of the Messiah as the Premillennialist pictures." (The Basis

> of Millennial Faith Grand Rapids: Eerdmans, Floyd
> E. Hamilton, 1942) p.38).

The One-Thousand Years, or Millennium, is the future period of literally one thousand years' duration. The beginning is marked by "an angel coming down from heaven, holding in his hand the key to the bottomless pit and a great chain" (Revelation 20:1). The angel seizes hold of Satan, the dragon serpent, and throws him into the pit, sealing him shut for one thousand years. This is the first of six references in Revelation to the one-thousand-year duration of the Millennium.

Once the beast is sequestered, Christ will return to the earth in the Parousia, His second coming to earth, to establish the Millennial Kingdom. Being locked in the abyss, Satan will be unable to continue his deception of the people. He will be unable to disrupt the conversion of God's people, in particular, the Jews. The rebellious sinners who were not already killed during the judgments meted out in the prior seven years of the Great Tribulation will have been killed or will have died during the battle at Armageddon. Jesus told of the final judgment in His Olivet Discourse:

> "[31]When the Son of Man comes in his glory, and all the angels with him, then he will sit on his glorious throne. [32]Before him will be gathered all the nations, and he will separate people one from another as a shepherd separates the sheep from the goats. [33]And he will place the sheep on his right, but the goats on the left. [34]Then the King will say to those on his right, 'Come, you who are blessed by my Father, inherit the kingdom prepared for you from the foundation of the world. [35]For I was

hungry and you gave me food, I was thirsty and you gave me drink, I was a stranger and you welcomed me, [36]I was naked and you clothed me, I was sick and you visited me.' [37]Then the righteous will answer him, saying, 'Lord, when did we see you hungry and feed you, or thirsty and give you drink? [38]And when did we see you a stranger and welcome you, or naked and clothe you? [39]And when did we see you sick or in prison and visit you? [40]And the King will answer them, 'Truly, I say to you, as you did it to one of the least of these my brothers, you did it to me.' [41]Then he will say to those on his left, 'Depart from me, you cursed, into the eternal fire prepared for the devil and his angels. [42]For I was hungry and you gave me no food, I was thirsty and you gave me no drink, [43]I was a stranger and you did not welcome me, naked and you did not clothe me, sick and in prison and you did not visit me.' [44]Then they also will answer, saying, 'Lord, when did we see you hungry or thirsty or a stranger or naked or sick or in prison, and did not minister to you?' [45]Then he will answer them, saying truly, I say to you, as you did not do it to one of the least of these, you did not do it to me.' [46]And these will go away into eternal punishment, but the righteous into eternal life." (Matthew 25:31-46).

Revelation 20 begins "Then I saw"

"As it frequently does in Revelation, the phrase "And I saw" indicates chronological progression. The location of the passage in the chronological flow of Revelation is consistent with a Premillennial view of the kingdom. After the tribulation Christ will return and set up His kingdom, followed by the new heavens and the new earth (21:1). The millennial kingdom comes after Christ's second coming but before establishing of the new heavens and new earth." (Because the Time is

Near", John MacArthur, Moody Publishers, Chicago, 2007, p.297)

The millennial kingdom will be ruled by the King of Kings and Lord of Lords, Jesus Christ. Christ will be assisted by His angels who come down with Him from heaven. Christ's angels will include the believers who were beheaded in His name, those who refused to worship the beast or take his mark on their forehead or hand, and all tribulation martyrs. John names the resurrection saints as the "first resurrection". This group is also referred to as the "resurrection of the righteous" in Luke 14:14, Acts 24:15, and the "resurrection of life" in John 5:29. The first resurrection will be the resurrection of the blessed who will reign with Christ on earth for the one-thousand-year millennium. They will compose the "royal priesthood" in 1 Peter 2:9. They will reign on earth with Christ for the millennium. The rest of the dead will not come to life until the millennium has ended.

All will change dramatically when Satan is released from the bottomless pit at the end of the millennium. The final assault by sinners will take place. Satan's army of sinners will have grown exponentially in numbers during the millennium. Despite living in a time of peace ruled by Jesus the Christ, many people will still love sin. Some will turn away from sin and come to Christ, but many will not and will reject Christ. It will be a tragic commentary on the depravity of humanity. When Satan is released from bondage, he will gather the sinners into a new rebellious army. They will "deceive the nations which are in the four corners of the earth" (Revelation 20:8).

"He will raise a signal for the nations and will assemble the banished of Israel, and gather the dispersed of Judah from the four corners of the earth." (Isaiah 11:12)

Despite it being hard to visualize, this final battle is part of God's plan. Satan and the rebels who will follow him are under God's control. John names this army of Satan "Gog and Magog", after the armies that will attack Israel during the Great Tribulation (Ezekiel 38–39). Gog and Magog likely describe the sinners who gather from all nations to fight—and lose—the final war in human history. Some believe that these chapters in Ezekiel describe the climactic battle at the end of the millennium. However, Ezekiel writes of the army that perished on Israel's mountains, while Revelation 20:9 describes rebels who are defeated on a "broad plain."

Gog is used in Scripture as a general reference to enemies of the people of God. Another view is that Gog, as used in verse 8 of Revelation 20, is a reference to the leader of Satan's army. Some believe Magog to be the descendants of Noah, referencing Genesis 10:2. Whoever they are, it is certain that they are sinners who will join forces to fight the final war of human history. What is stunning is that John saw in his vision that the rebels who will join to fight Christ will be greater in number than the sands of the sea. Gog and Magog are the oppressors of Israel. They will swarm to the home of the throne of the Messiah, the city of Jerusalem, to engage in war. Gog and Magog will be destroyed by fire. As was the battle of Armageddon, Christ and His followers will crush the evil forces. This final destruction of Satan's forces will be immediate and complete. They will be killed en masse in an instant, and their souls will go to hell for eternity. Satan will be cast into the lake of fire and brimstone to join the beast and the false prophet for eternity (Matthew 25:46; 2 Thessalonians 1:9), never to see the Lord, but to live in incomprehensible darkness and agony.

Judgment Before the Great White Throne

[11]Then I saw a great white throne and him who was seated on it. From his presence earth and sky fled away, and no place was found for them. [12]And I saw the dead, great and small, standing before the throne, and books were opened. Then another book was opened, which is the book of life. And the dead were judged by what was written in the books, according to what they had done. [13]And the sea gave up the dead who were in it, Death. and Hades gave up the dead who were in them, and they were judged, each one of them, according to what they had done. [14]Then Death and Hades were thrown into the lake of fire. This is the second Death, the lake of fire. [15]And if anyone's name was not found written in the book of life he was thrown into the lake of fire.

White symbolizes holiness, purity, and authority. The great white throne represents the wisdom and purity of the Ancient of Days (Daniel 7:9). We are given an early glimpse of God's great white throne of judgment in Revelation 4:2–8, where it is surrounded by the twenty-four elders clothed in white. John saw both flashes of lightning symbolizing God's judgment and a rainbow symbolizing His merciful promises. In Revelation 20:11–12, Jesus Christ is seated on His throne. Representing purity, Christ's throne is great and white. God the Father and Jesus His Son share the throne, but it is Jesus who sits on it. The role of Jesus is to judge all sinners. Thus, Christ is at the forefront in Revelation.

The earth and the sky were gone, having been destroyed in the final defeat of Satan. In Revelation 20:12–15, John next sees the second resurrection, the resurrection of the dead, who will stand before the Lord Jesus. Every person will be returned to their former bodily life and then be judged. The books of judgment are opened. The book of life will then be opened. This book is the record of our lives and our actions. The Lord God keeps track of every person's deeds and actions (Daniel 7:10; Romans 2:6–11).

Revelation 3:5 informs us that the "one who conquers" is clothed in white garments and, because of trusting in Jesus Christ, will have his name recorded in the Book of Life and will thus be saved. The dead of the land and of the sea will be raised from their graves for judgment. They will be judged by their deeds, according to "what was written in the books". "Death and Hades" will be thrown into the lake of fire, along with anyone whose name is "not found written in the Book of Life," the record of God's elected ones. All who are not listed in this book will be eternally damned. Not all eternal punishment will be the same. In Luke 12:47–48, we learn that there will be degrees of punishment in hell. However, hell will never be anything less than horrific.

> "Because he has fixed the day on which he will judge the world in righteousness by a man who he has appointed; and of this he has given assurance to all by raising him from the dead." (Acts 17:31).

"[47]And the servant that knew his master's will but did not get ready or act according to his will, will receive a severe beating. [48]But the one who did not know, and did what deserved a beating, will receive a light beating. Everyone to whom much was given, of him much will be required, and from him to who they entrusted much, they will demand more." (Luke 12:47-48).

Death will be erased for those whose names are written in the Book of Life. They will enter the New Jerusalem and be saved. The unsaved, whose names are not recorded in the Book of Life, will face eternal condemnation and be thrown into the lake of fire.

Chapter 23

The New Heaven and the New Earth

The New Heaven and the New Earth

There will be sin during the millennium

21Then I saw a new heaven and a new earth, for the first heaven and the first earth had passed away, and the sea was no more. [2]And I saw the holy city, new Jerusalem, coming down out of the heaven from God, prepared as a bride adorned for her husband. [3]And I heard a loud voice from the throne saying, "Behold, the dwelling place of God is with man. He will dwell with them, and they will be his people, and God himself will be with them as their God. [4]He will wipe away every tear from their eyes, and Death shall be no more, neither shall there be mourning, nor crying, nor pain anymore, for the former things have passed away." [5]And he who was seated on the throne said, "Behold, I am making all things new." Also he said, "Write this down, for these words are trustworthy and true." [6]And he said to me, "It is done! I am the Alpha and the Omega, the beginning and the end. To the thirsty I will give from the spring of the water of life without payment. [7]The one who conquers will have this heritage, and I will be his God and he will be my son. [8]But as for the cowardly, the faithless, the detestable, as for murderers, the sexually immoral, sorcerers, idolaters, and all liars, their portion will be in the lake that burns with fire and sulfur, which is the second Death."

How often have we wondered what heaven will be like? Jesus told John what heaven would be like, and John was caught up to heaven and allowed to see certain things. The description is brief—perhaps because we are not yet able to grasp the full glory that believers will experience there. John was shown three heavens. He saw things so spectacular that he could not write them down and was not permitted to reveal them.

> "[3]And I know that this man was caught up into paradise – whether in the body or out of the body I do not know, God knows - [4]and he heard things that cannot be told, which man may not be utter." (2 Corinthians 12:3-4).

God declared in Isaiah 65:17, "For behold, I create new heavens and a new earth, and the former things shall not be remembered or come into mind." In Isaiah 66:22, we read, "For as the new heavens and the new earth that I make shall remain before me, says the Lord, so shall your offspring and your name remain."

In Revelation 21:1–4, John saw a new heaven and a new earth. He saw the New Jerusalem, which tells us that there will be a new heaven and a new earth. The first heaven and earth will "pass away", and there will be no more sea. There will be a new and glorious holy city—the New Jerusalem—that will come down from heaven, as foretold in Revelation 21:2–21. The culmination will be a new, intimate relationship between God and His people, as introduced in Revelation 21:22–27. God will "dwell among" men, and "they will be His people" (Revelation 21:3). The saved will no longer "groan… in pain of childbirth" (Romans 8:21–22).

The believers and the angels will worship God night and day. The New Jerusalem will have no temple, no sun, and no moon. God's glory will give light to His people. All nations and people will walk by God's light, and uncleanness will never defile the city. The new heavens and the new earth are God's promise to His church (Isaiah 65:13, 17; 2 Peter 3:12–13).

Our earthly bodies are composed of about ninety percent water, and the earth is seventy-five percent water. In the new heaven and the new earth, we will have new, heavenly bodies that will be very different. We will need no water, and the earth will have no water. The only water in heaven will be the "water of life." "Death, where is thy sting?" (1 Corinthians 15:55–57).

> The first heaven is the atmosphere, the air we breathe…The second heaven is outer space where the sun, the moons, the planets, and the galaxies are located. The third heaven in the Bible is where God resides. It's where you and I and our loved ones, if we're Christians, go temporarily when we die. This is the heaven Paul had in mind when he said he preferred "to be absent from the body and to be at home with the Lord" (2 Corinthians 5:8). It was also the third heaven that Paul "was caught up to" for a momentary visit (2 Corinthians 12:2). No one knows where the third heaven is. But there is the mistake many Christians make about the third heaven: they think that wherever God is, that's going to be our eternal dwelling place. Christians say, "I'm going to be home with the Lord. I'm going to live up there someplace forever". It may surprise you that this is not the case. The Bible says the third heaven is

> only a temporary place for us. When we die, we go wherever God is to be with Him. We're aware, we're awake, and we're conscious – but that's only a temporary place. The fourth heaven is the new heaven and the new earth that have yet to be created. It's going to be centered mainly right here on this earth. Yes, this earth is going to be our final dwelling place, not the third heaven where God dwells. The Bible is very clear about our ultimate destination. The psalmist said, "Those who wait on the Lord, they will inherit the land" (Psalm 37:9), that is, the earth." (Final Conquest, Dr. Robert Jeffress, Pathway to Victory, pp. 317-318).

Scripture is unequivocal that there will be a new heaven and a new earth with a capital city. "For he was looking forward to the city that has foundations, whose designer and builder was God." (Hebrews 11:10). The architect of the new city is clear. It will be named Jerusalem—the third city so named. The first Jerusalem was Jerusalem of old, and the second will be the restored Jerusalem, where believers will live with Christ during the millennial kingdom.

> And he who was seated on the throne said, "Behold, I am making all things new. Also, he said, "Write this down, for these words are trustworthy and true." And he said to me, "It is done! I am the Alpha and the Omega, the beginning and the end. To the thirsty I will give from the spring of the water of life without payment." (Revelation 21:5-6).

In Revelation 1:8, Jesus, our Lord God, told us that He is the Alpha and the Omega. He is also the architect and builder of the new city. He tells us in John 14:3 that He will prepare a place—a new home—for us. Jesus tells us in Revelation 21:7

that he who conquers, meaning to overcome and to persevere, will be the son of God, our Lord and Savior. His name will be in the book of life, and he will wear white garments. All that is required of us in order to enter into the new Jerusalem is to truly believe in Christ our Savior, for He is the Son of God. To be clear, Jesus tells us in verse 8 who will not enter heaven: the cowardly, faithless, detestable, murderers, sexually immoral, sorcerers, idolaters, and all liars—these will burn in the lake of fire and sulfur.

Every person ever born, except for Jesus Christ, is a sinner. Sinners who repent will enter heaven. We are all called to repent and turn away from sin.

> Let's be perfectly clear: neither homosexuality, adultery, fornication, nor idolatry is something to celebrate. They are abominations to God, and those who practice these things have no place in His Kingdom." (Final Conquest, Dr. Robert Jeffress, Pathway to Victory, pp. 322).

Believers are saved, and all their sins are wiped away by their confession to Almighty God and their belief in the saving Blood of our Lord Jesus Christ. If we do this and truly believe, we are secure in our salvation and our entrance into heaven. As Paul wrote to the Philippians in 3:20, "our citizenship is in heaven."

The new Jerusalem will be so beautiful that we are incapable of imagining its full glory. We do not need to imagine for ourselves, for we are told what it will be like beginning in verse 9.

The New Jerusalem

[9]Then came one of the seven angels who had the seven bowls full of the seven last plagues and spoke to me, saying, "Come, I will show you the Bride, the wife of the Lamb." [10]And he carried me away in the Spirit to the great, high mountain, and showed me the holy city Jerusalem coming down out of the heaven from God, [11]having the glory of God, its radiance like a most rare jewel, like a jasper, clear as crystal. [12]It had a great, high wall, with twelve gates, and at the gates twelve angels, and on the gates the names of the twelve tribes of the sons of Israel were inscribed – [13]on the east three gates, on the north three gates, on the south three gates and on the west three gates. [14]And the wall of the city had twelve foundations, and on them were the twelve names of the twelve apostles of the Lamb. [15]And the one who spoke with me had a measuring rod of gold to measure the city and its gates and walls. [16]The city lies foursquare, its length the same as its width. And he measured the city with his rod, 12,000 stadia. Its length and width and height are equal. [17]He also measured its wall, 144 cubits by human measurement, which is also an angel's measurement. [18]The wall was built of jasper, while the city was pure gold, like clear glass. [19]The foundations of the wall of the city were adorned with every kind of jewel. The first was jasper, the second sapphire, the third agate, the fourth emerald, [20]the fifth onyx, the sixth carnelian the seventh chrysolite, the eight beryl, the nineth topaz, the tenth chrysoprase, the eleventh jacinth, the twelfth amethyst. [21]And the twelve gates were twelve pearls, each of the gates made of a single pearl, and the street of the city was pure gold, like transparent glass. [22]And I saw no temple in the city for its temple is the Lord God the Almighty and the Lamb.

[23]And the city has no need for sun or moon to shine on it, for the glory of God gives it light and its lamp is the Lamb. [24]By its light will the nations walk, and the kings of the earth will bring their glory into it, [25]and its gates will never be shut by day - and there will be no night there, [26]They will bring into it glory and honor of the nations. [27]But nothing unclean will ever enter it, nor will anyone who does what is detestable or false, but only those who are written in the Lamb's book of life.

An angel comes in Revelation 21:9 to show John the New Jerusalem, the bride of the Lamb. She is the holy city. The Lamb is Christ, and the residents are those of purified character. This vision also serves as a metaphor for the saved of all ages who will be forever united with the Lamb. Their marriage has taken place. John, who was imprisoned on the island of Patmos, was carried away in the Spirit by the angel so that he might see and record these sights. This was not a dream; this was John's lived experience. John saw the capital city and the glory of God brilliantly radiating from the New Jerusalem.

The residents of the city will not know sorrow, pain, illness, Death, or hunger. Being the saved church, they will dwell with God. The New Jerusalem will be massive in size—1,500 miles square and 660,000 stories tall. There will never again be a curse on the people. They will know only joy. Having a new relationship with God, they will see His face, for as saints of the New Jerusalem, they will be righteous and holy.

The city will be adorned with an uncountable number of precious stones that give light and beauty. The stones mark God's covenant with His church. Angels will be stationed to attend to God and His glory and to serve God's people. There will be twelve gates, each named for the twelve apostles and the twelve tribes of the sons of Israel. Her gates will remain always open.

Chapter 24

The River of Life

The River of Life

22Then the angel showed me the river of the water of life, bright as crystal, flowing from the throne of God and of the Lamb ²through the middle of the street of the city; also, on either side of the river, the tree of life with its twelve kinds of fruit, yielding its fruit each month. The leaves of the tree were for the healing of the nations. ³No longer will there be anything accursed, but the throne of God and of the Lamb will be in it, and his servants will worship him. ⁴They will see his face, and his name will be on their foreheads. ⁵And night will be no more. They will need no light of lamp or sun, for the Lord God will be their light, and they will reign forever and ever.

Water is a symbol or metaphor of eternal life. The Garden of Eden had a river with four forks. In Revelation 22:1–2, we read of a river that was "bright as crystal, flowing from the throne of God and of the Lamb through the city." Next to the river stands the tree of life, bearing twelve fruits for the twelve months. The fruits heal the nations. This is the tree of life that creation first saw in the Garden of Eden. The curse has now forever ended. Bond-servants will serve, worship, and see the face of God, whose name shall be on their foreheads. There is no night or day, and no lights, because the Lord will reign and illuminate forever and ever.

Jesus Is Coming

⁶And he said to me, "These words are trustworthy and true. And the Lord, the God of the Spirits of the prophets, has sent his angel to show his servants what must soon take place."

⁷"And behold, I am coming soon. Blessed is the one who keeps the words of the prophecy of this book."

⁸I, John, am the one who heard and saw these things. And when I heard and saw them, I fell down to worship at the feet of the angel who showed them to me, ⁹but he said to me, "You must not do that! I am a fellow servant with you and your brothers the prophets, and with those who keep the words of this book. Worship God."

¹⁰And he said to me, "Do not seal up the works of the prophecy of this book, for the time is near. ¹¹Let the evildoer still do evil, and filthy still be filthy, and the righteous still do right, and the holy still be holy."

¹²"Behold, I am coming soon, bringing my recompense with me, to repay each one for what he has done. ¹³I am the Alpha and the Omega, the first and the last, the beginning and the end."

¹⁴Blessed are those who wash their robes, so that they may have the right to the tree of life and that they may enter the city by the gates. ¹⁵Outside are the dogs and sorcerers and the sexually immoral and murderers and idolaters, and everyone who loves and practices falsehood.

¹⁶ "I, Jesus, have sent my angel to testify to you about these things for the churches. I am the root and the descendant of David, the bright morning star,"

¹⁷The Spirit and the Bride say, "Come." And let the one who hears say, "Come." And let the one who is thirsty come; let the one who desires take the water of life without price.

[18]I warn everyone who hears the words of the prophecy of this book: if anyone adds to them, God will add to him the plagues described in this book, [19] and if anyone takes away from the words of the book of this prophecy, God will take away his share in the tree of life and in the holy city, which are described in this book. [20]He who testifies to these things says,
"Surely I am coming soon." Amen. Come, Lord Jesus!
[21]The grace of the Lord Jesus be with all. Amen.

The angel reassured John that "these words are trustworthy and true. And the Lord, the God of the spirits of the prophets, has sent his angel to show his servants what must soon take place. And behold, I am coming soon. Blessed is the one who keeps the words of the prophecy of this book." (Revelation 22:6–7). Even he who reads this prophecy is blessed.

Revelation 22:14 instructs us that "blessed are those who wash their robes". This wording is not used in the King James Version, published in 1611, which reads, "Blessed are they that do his commandments". The difference is significant, as the KJV translation implies that our good works are what gain us entrance into heaven.

Biblical scholars today believe the KJV translation is in error because the original Greek manuscripts read, "Blessed are those who wash their robes." I believe this translation aligns with the original text and is fully consistent with the widely accepted doctrine that we gain entrance to heaven by our faith in our Lord Jesus Christ, who died on the cross that we may live. It is by grace, and grace alone, that we are saved.

"Revelation 22:10 refers to a season or era (with the word Kairos). In other words, the season of Christ's coming is near. We are living in the last period of time before the rapture of the church. This is the church age, when God has temporarily set aside the Jewish people to allow Gentiles to come in and share in God's blessing. This final period of time could end at any moment, even today…. There is such a process for you and me, a time in the future when our relationship with God will be fixed for all eternity. This will come either at your Death or at the rapture of the church. The moment you die, all opportunity for change in your life is over. That's what Revelation 22:11 is saying. The moment you die, if you are practicing righteousness, you will continue practicing righteousness for all eternity in a beautiful relationship with God. But if you die apart from faith in Christ, you will spend eternity apart from God, rebelling against Him in hell forever." (Final Conquest, Dr. Robert Jeffress, Pathway to Victory, p. 334-335).

The Bible closes by stating its truthfulness:

[18]"I warn everyone who hears the words of prophecy of this book: if anyone adds to them, God will add to him the plagues described in this book, [19]and if anyone takes away from the words of this book of this prophecy, God will take away his share in the tree of life and in the holy city, which are described in this book." (Revelation 22: 18-19)

As we read in the gospels, we must watch and be ready.

"[14]Blessed are those who wash their robes, so that they may have the right to the tree of life and that they may

enter the city by the gates. [15]Outside are the dogs and sorcerers and the secularly immoral and murderers and idolaters and everyone who loves and practices falsehood. I, Jesus, have sent my angel to testify to you about these things for the churches. I am the root and the descendant of David, the bright morning star."
(Revelation 22:14-16)

"He who testifies to these things says, "Surely I am coming soon. Amen. Come, Lord Jesus!"
(Revelation 22: 20)

No other book of the Bible carries a special blessing to the reader. These are truly our Lord and Savior's last recorded words to us, and He is coming for His church soon. Are you ready?

References

- The Holy Bible, English Standard Version, Crossway, Wheaton, Illinois, 2001.

- Final Conquest, A Verse-by-Verse Study of the Book of Revelation, Pathway to Victory, Dallas, Texas, 2020, Dr. Robert Jeffress.

- Bible Prophecy Made Simple, Pathway to Victory, Dallas, Texas, 2020, Dr. Robert Jeffress.

- Because The Time IS Near, Moody Publishers, Chicago, 2007, John MacArthur.

- Revelation, Moody Publishers, Chicago, Illinois, 2011, John F. Walvoord, Edited by Philip E. Rawley & Mark Hitchcock.

- The Book of Revelation, The New International Commentary on the New Testament, Grand Rapids, Eerdmans, 1977.

- Revelation, An Exegetical Commentary, 1-7 and 8-22, Moody Publishers, Chicago, Illinois, 1992, Robert L. Thomas.

- The New International Commentary on the New Testament, The Book of Revelation Revised Edition,

Dennis Mahoney

William B. Eerdmans Publishing Company, Grand
Rapids, Michigan / Cambridge U.K., 1977, First
Edition, Robert H. Mounce.